good deed rain

Allen Frost is author of 59 books

Novels Featuring Marconi & Cronco:

The Robotic Age
A Field of Cabbages
Cosmonaut
Half a Giraffe
Neptunalia

NEPTUNALIA

NEPTUNALIA © 2023
Allen Frost, Good Deed Rain
Bellingham, Washington
ISBN: 978-1-0880-8444-1

Writing: Allen Frost
Art: Aaron Gunderson
Cover Production: Priya Shalauta
Quotes:
Batman Victorious, A Columbia Serial, 1949.
Richard Hugo, *A Trout in the Milk: A Composite Portrait of Richard Hugo*, Edited by Jack Myers, Confluence Press, ID, 1982.
W.S. Merwin, "Blue" from *The Miner's Pale Children*, Atheneum, NY, 1970.
Apple: TFK!

"He was too absorbed in his scientific experiments in a secret workshop"

   —Batman

NEPTUNALIA

by Allen Frost

Illustrated by Aaron Gunderson

Good Deed Rain ◊ Bellingham, Washington ◊ 2023

"There's nothing gradual about anything in Seattle. Everything is dramatic and dark. The predominant colors are gray and a kind of black-green of the pine trees."

—Richard Hugo

INTRODUCTION

This is a tribute to Neptune. I've been wanting to thank the Neptune Theatre. Every age of the empire will be remembered for something. Far away as ancient Rome, my high school days are mostly to be recalled for seeing movies in Seattle's Neptune palace. I just recalled an early novel *When You Smile You Let in Light* starts with our hero there. I like the balcony, below the projection booth, just under the moving light. It might seem that immortal Neptune doesn't play that big a part in this book, but that's not true. I assure you, every sentence is another wave in the ocean. Neptune creaks evermore on his rocking chair, underwater in Green Lake, seeing all.

—AF, December 13, 2022

In the deepest part of blue one of the immortals
lives alone.

—W.S. Merwin

CHAPTERS

The Counterfeit Reality

CHAPTER 1
The Times of Rome

It's a well-known fact to anyone who works at the Neptune Theatre that there is a gorilla ghost in the cellar. That's the reason for the chained, padlocked basement door. Whether it was true or not, the rumor kept people from exploring downstairs, where an underground river was allowed to flow and create catacombs below. Here's how the legend goes…A hundred years ago, a jungle explorer appeared on the stage. He stood in a spotlight surrounded by tropical plants and palm tree cutouts. While his voice boomed across the rows, a magic lantern showed pictures in blazing color behind him. Then his assistant brought out cages—chattering monkeys, a lion, a ten-foot snake and that infamous gorilla. It's said that the giant ape got loose and clawed up the red stage curtains trying to get to the rafters. The audience was screaming, shoving in the aisles, as the explorer pulled out a revolver and fired and down the ape plummeted. That's the rumor—nobody dared go into the cellar to find out if it was true—but to this day you can still see the gorilla-shaped patch on the floor. That wasn't the only historic moment in the Neptune Theatre, there were others, and other ghosts too…and someone in the cellar, unseen since the times of Rome.

CHAPTER 2
The Neptune Theatre

How does a god become forgotten? New ones get created. Names change. Even Neptune knew that—he used to be called Poseidon in a previous empire. Time changes everything. If he had fallen out of sight that wasn't surprising. Anyway, he wasn't totally forgotten. He still had a palace named after him…Built in 1921, The Neptune Theatre was a church for a lot of people in Seattle. I myself was one of the congregation. When I was in high school, I would be there every week for movies. Every night was a shared prayer with Bergman, Fellini, Woody Allen, Ozu, all the actors, and behind one of those golden masks glowing eyes along the theater's wall was an actual god. It must have been a spell. Seeing those movies changed my life.

I don't know exactly how it happened, I was away at school for four years and then other things happened, and all the while Seattle was turning into a whole other city. Places I used to go turned into ghosts. I've been past the building with its green neon sign, The Neptune Theatre is still there, but I haven't gone in since I heard it stopped showing movies. No more sealight shining over the chairs. I'm glad Neptune got to experience that palace— imagine what it must have been like to be part of all the people coming and going for all those years, waiting for the houselights to dim so another new movie could begin. When Neptune left it was easy for him to go, he just slid into the gutter and flowed.

Neptune was done with the movies, their Golden Age was over, and he was ready to leave Seattle. As long as it was raining, he could lean on his trident up and down the seven hills of the city, the locks, the bridges, the monorail, the trees and water. He needed the water. Whatever form he took, however he survived down through the ages, was dependent on water.

The rain took him to Puget Sound, spilling him among the piers, the barnacles and blue oil slicks, the loading docks, the choppy green waves, the heavy din of propellers, ferry boats and freighters. He swam from the land and wove between the islands. When Neptune arrived at my town, I was working fulltime at Poseidon Fish n Chips. I was writing my first book, *Saint Lemonade*. I'm always writing a book. I'm not sure why, certainly not to make money, you can't make a living that way, simply put I do it because I have to. It makes my life complete. I guess Neptune knew that when he climbed ashore and went looking for me.

CHAPTER 3
Faith

Neptune was residing in a fountain outside the Key Bank downtown. Staking it out, you might say. It seemed that observing was the god's new function. People on the street would go back and forth, walking, driving, riding the bus. Did Neptune mean anything to them? Whatever they were doing, whatever their story, they would only be a reflection in the fountain. The water stayed like glass unless someone threw in a coin, or some sort of litter blew onto it and sailed across.

He didn't expect to be seen by anyone but me. A few pennies surrounded him. He was a worn nickel in a pool. Gods can be whatever they want to be, he was confident this form would do. I guess he knew I was a cheapskate. Every payday I went to the bank to deposit my check and like clockwork, on the way out I would stop at the fountain.

I like watching water, I always have, it's a mystery the way another world is living in there. Neptune lured me to the fountain where I would stare like a two-year old looking for fish. It would have been easy for Neptune to be a Chinook salmon, that would surely get my attention, but he knew five cents would do the trick. I spotted the silver coin, rolled up my sleeve and fished it out and brought it home. It was an old one, 1956. So it ended up on the windowsill in a little saucer of water. I just thought it looked better underwater, but it was Neptune controlling me to do that. He breathes in water. From that saucer, he got a chance to see me at work, he witnessed how I live to write books and he was pleased.

Neptune had to make sure I was devoted, that I wasn't one of those people who only said they were an author, and he had to make sure I suffered for it, was tested and tried, and through it all he watched the titles roll out…*Town in a Cloud*, *The Orphanage of Abandoned Teenagers*, *Homeless Sutra*, *Island Air*, *Something Bright*, *Forest and Field*…more than fifty of them before he was ready to make himself known.

I wasn't surprised by Neptune's appearance,

like I said, we've been aware since those green eyes watched me while the movie was going. Neptune knew me from then and he had faith that those movies I saw long ago would stay with me and make me a storyteller too. He was right. It worked. After all these years, I'm writing Neptune's book.

CHAPTER 4
Prayer

When I saw James Dean in *East of Eden*, Neptune was watching as always from the mask on the wall. It's possible I was alert to that, I must have been, why wouldn't I be? I'd seen enough Charlie Chan movies to believe that can happen— eyes behind masks, secret panels and passages, mysteries and wonders that could be projected by magic light. I lived for it. You could find me in those schooldays driving at night in a little white Toyota Corolla, radio jumping between KJET and KCMU or the oldies station on AM, going from screen to screen.

Crest Cinema, The Varsity, The Guild 45th, The Ridgemont, The Seven Gables, The Grand Illusion. At The Egyptian, I was lucky enough to see Robert Wise and Dennis Hopper in person for a double feature of *Rebel Without a Cause* and *The Last Movie.* Unbelievable! Neptune couldn't miss it either. He hurried along the copper lines running underground so he could appear in the water fountain if you pressed the button. You would think a God could do a little better than that, but that's the way it was in today's age. The halls of the Crest were lined with lobby cards and photographs. Some dim lights shone down from the ceiling. I never bought the popcorn, but I remember its spot in the corner front window and how it steamed up the glass. Upstairs at the Harvard Exit was a big silver urn full of orange spice tea for free. I got a full paper cup and wandered into *Down By Law.* I know it seems foolhardy to drive into nostalgia like this, longing for the dream of a better world, but I'm pretty sure that's what the gods are looking for in a prayer.

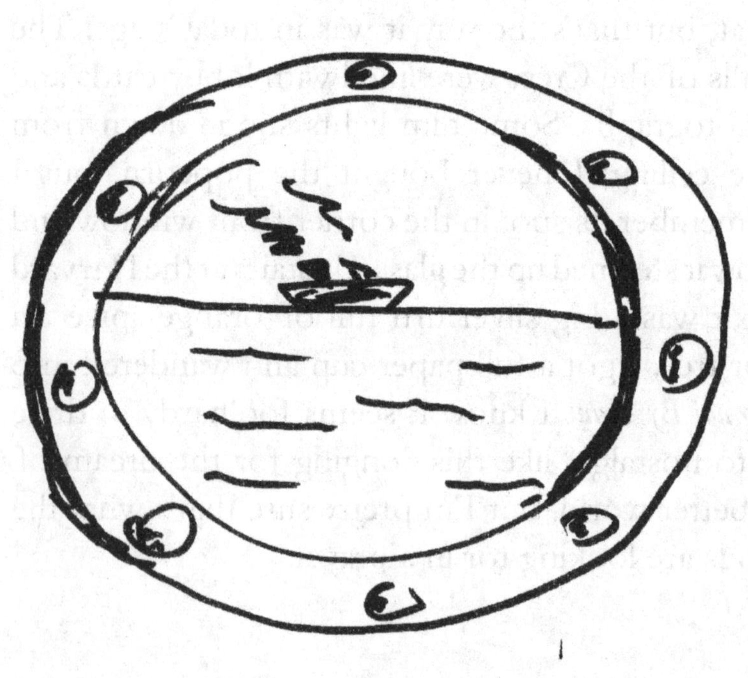

CHAPTER 5
At the Center of a Wheel

That's enough about me though, there's a lot more going on and it's time to get back to it now. This is where Neptune wants to belong. At the center of a wheel, in a story that revolves around God. As I understand it, put simply, this is the story of someone who doesn't want to be forgotten. Not unlike Hercules, I've been given a labor as real and challenging as stealing the apples of the Hesperides—to bring Neptune's name back into light. I don't mind writing it, Neptune chose me because that's what I do. I get words and put them together in rows and slowly it's built. This book will be Neptune's new palace.

CHAPTER 6:
Paperclip Hero

The Great Marconi lost his leg in a tragic magic act [see *The Robotic Age*—ED]. It happened years ago, don't worry, you would never know it, he's alright now. Everything's fine. He got a new leg. Ironically though, his robot companion Cronco suffered the same pegleg fate. What an unkind lesson: what's here today may not be here tomorrow. It was their lot. Marconi knew that's the way it goes in a life devoted to prestidigitation.

Everything jumped. Marconi sat in a tram near a boy. All the windows were black, there was nothing to see but their reflections. The rails clacked, the walls shook. They didn't know each other, this old magician and the boy, but they had been neighbors for the last half an hour. They met at the dentist office. They were both wearing medals from their experience there. The medal was a circle of gold foil with red, white and blue paper ribbons stapled on. They were handmade by the secretary, identical except for the message she wrote on the gold. The boy's medal read HERO—he made it through his dentist appointment bravely. The old man next to him wore a medal that said CRYBABY.

For the next three minutes they were traveling under the bay. An ocean of water flowed overhead, a hundred feet of fish and seals and seaweed forests. Marconi crossed his leg and waved his shoe. Three minutes seems a long time with nothing to do. The boy was holding a small wooden box with a glass window. Inside of it, the heroic boy guided a silver ball-bearing carefully through a maze. Marconi rolled his eyes. Real entertainment was called for. It was time for some magic.

Marconi reached into his tuxedo pocket and tossed something small and shiny into the center aisle.

The boy took his eyes from the game for a second, long enough to be uninterested in the world outside the wooden box.

Undeterred, Marconi raised a finger and pointed at the paperclip he had thrown. As if linked to that trembling finger by unseen string, the paperclip twitched. Marconi stirred the air and the paperclip hitched itself on its side and stood on end. This miniature miracle didn't cause a rush of attention, but Marconi's magic seldom did. He nudged the boy with an elbow.

"Hey! What are you doing?" The ball in the wooden box rattled freely.

Still pointing at the aisle, the old magician chuffed, "Look…"

It took a moment for the boy to tell what he was looking at. A paperclip. A bit of the ordinary floor population, sharing space with a torn newspaper, a penny, a barrette, a mashed paper cup. They were forgotten things. The old man could have made the paperclip float and it wouldn't have impressed. If there was an elephant on the tram, he could have levitated it, but you can only make do with what you have on hand. The boy went back to his game. Maybe if Marconi could have explained, drawn the whole car in with a circus sounding voice, but his mouth was stuffed with cotton, and heroics were the last thing anyone expected from a man wearing a CRYBABY ribbon.

CRY BABY

CHAPTER 7
Ahead of the Future

A hundred years ago you might have heard the steady, rhythmic sound of a peglegged whaler clopping his way on the cobblestones up from the sea. The sea is still there, flat and blue on a spring day, but whales are rare and the men who once hunted them are all gone. Time has passed and a robot is walking on the sidewalk.

Poor Cronco took a spill down some rickety apartment stairs [see *Half a Giraffe*—ED] and has been limping for weeks, using a crutch like a mechanical Long John Silver. He and Marconi were saving money to get a new leg. It was slow work. Every Saturday, Cronco went to the park with drawing supplies. It wasn't easy for Marconi and Cronco to do magic, there was no vaudeville circuit anymore, they had to look for other jobs, it was the way of the world. Honestly though, Cronco didn't miss the stage, he wanted to be an artist, he was tired of magic and the trouble it got him into.

Every limping step he took would remind him of that. After all he had been through, he could use a new Cadillac heart as well. He didn't want to remember that awful moment falling at The Oxford Apartments, so he deleted it from his memory bank. It was easy for a robot to forget bad things. He had no idea how he lost his right leg. Along the way he supposed he had blown a circuit or been hit by lightning, and it just fell off. For now a wooden leg would have to do.

It turned out to be a good thing Cronco was on Astor Street at that exact moment. Heroes are created by the simple act of being in the right place at the right time. Just past the oak tree, in the shadowed driveway to Santy's Upholstery, The Great Marconi was leading a floating dog.

Cronco could tell right away that something was wrong. It wasn't the sort of animal balloon Marconi would sell at the zoo for a dollar, it was a real dog and it was floating ten feet off the ground, pulling the old man across the lawn. Marconi bravely tried to hold onto that leash, but Cronco could predict what was going to happen, and then it did. The dog blew out of Marconi's hands. Up it went, kicking its legs, swimming in the air, over a telephone wire. Cronco watched it turn into a dot.

It took Cronco some more crutching to get to the path.

Marconi waved his magic wand at the sky but the dog was gone. "What's happened to my magic?" he moaned, "That used to be the simplest illusion and now look what I've done."

"I am sorry you lost your dog." Cronco may have been an eight-foot robot, but he had been programmed to be comforting and to help whenever he could. "Will you allow me to retrieve him?"

"How?" The sky was nothing but clouds.

"I have radar, I can see much further, I can track it and locate its destination." The robot made it sound easy. Cronco left his easel and paper and paints on the sidewalk with Marconi and promised he would catch the dog. He left Astor and headed southwest, past the shops and the big Trident Imports. In some towns it might seem a little unusual to see a one-legged robot trudging along, but Cronco lived here, he fit right in with the parking meters, the lampposts, the newspaper machine, and the silver mailbox on the corner.

Adjusting for wind velocity and direction, Cronco was able to calculate the dog's trajectory. It was headed for the harbor, specifically Marine Park. This robot wasn't built for speed and having to hobble on a pegleg only slowed him more, but he was confident. That was another of his built-in circuits—Confidence—although it was known to short out sometimes. Plus, he was getting to be an old robot. He was built at a time when it was assumed the automaton would be humanity's best hope and factories churned out larger-than-life mechanical people to work in the mines or babysit or do odd jobs. They were the future today…Not quite…When Cronco Industries went bankrupt, they sold their product for scrap. Cronco #501322 was one of the few of his kind remaining.

He carefully managed his way over the railroad tracks. His body tipped and rattled. He was anxious to get across, there were horror stories of robots being hit by trains. Nothing left but a flat outline. He shuddered. He couldn't help it. His Fear circuit was activated.

On Laurel Street, a blue and white delivery truck chimed past. It was filled with glass bottles of Wooden Water that rang like bells.

CHAPTER 8
The Flying Dog

The Great Marconi, Dogwalker.

That's how he was listed in the *Herald*. He was determined to earn the money to buy Cronco a new leg, one that was meant for a robot, one that fit. No more table legs or roofbeams. Marconi was pulled by five dogs on the sidewalk to the store where he found a rare vintage leg from a Cronco #501335. There was only one slight flaw—it was a left leg—could a missing right leg be replaced by a left one? "No matter!" Marconi assured the shop owner, "Put it on hold, I'll soon have your payment." He sold balloons at the zoo, and he walked dogs at the park, holding two handfuls of leashes. Typically, Marconi didn't like to work with animals. It's true his magic act used to have a rabbit. Until it escaped, that rabbit was a real crowd-pleaser…He never should have left it in a top-hat on a picnic table.

Marconi often met his robot friend at the park. They'd find a bench and Cronco would put aside his paints and tourist portraits and Marconi would tie off his dogs. It gave them a chance to rest. Only yesterday Marconi pointed at the ground.

"Cronco, have you observed the ants toiling at our feet?"

The big robot looked next to his metal shoe.

"Not one of them seems to know the meaning of a straight line…"

They watched them for a while then Marconi sighed, "But I suppose we're not so very different. Look at all our sidesteps and backtracks and pitfalls we endure just to get from Point A to Point B."

Today they had no time for philosophy. This time the sight of Cronco meant that maybe he found Marconi's missing flying dog. "Cronco!" the old man shouted as he left the parking lot, pulled by his dogs across the grass.

Ahead of them, the big robot was standing below a tree, tipped back, looking up into the leaves. Marconi worried something might have gone wrong with Cronco again. Only a couple weeks before, there had been some trouble with the robot's circuitry. His Artist circuit usually allowed him to create masterpieces, but he got bumped or scrambled or somehow went haywire and he was drawings hideous caricatures and babbling like a broken radio. It was frightening, so unlike the robot's past behavior.

"Cronco," Marconi said, "Are you okay?"

The beagle in Marconi's dog pack started to yowl. The others joined in barking and yapping at something stuck and thrashing high in the tree. As Marconi was dragged closer, he could see what it was, but he couldn't believe his eyes—Cronco had performed an illusion worthy of Houdini—there was a dog in a tree!

Cronco held his silver arms outstretched, ready to catch the flying dog if it fell. With Marconi and his pets gathered around, the robot explained, "Now that I have located it, I am not able to ascertain the most advantageous way of getting this animal to the ground."

A low seagull circled the tree. It shrieked once.

The dog in the tree gave a lunge and freed itself from the branches. Kicking its legs got it a few feet away from the tree. If it followed the white bird out to sea, Cronco couldn't go after it. Signaling with his waving arms didn't do any good. If only a salty breeze would blow it back, to tangle round the flagpole on the Leopold tower, they could lasso it down.

An ultrasonic sound stitched through the air. Cronco had to clap a hand over his tin ear. He could hear it of course, but the sound was meant for dogs—Marconi had a dog whistle. It was how he kept his parade together. Right away there were seven dogs hypnotized at his feet.

The sound worked with the flying dog too. It couldn't resist turning around. It swam down from the sky and as it paddled by, the robot pinched a claw on the trailing leash.

"That was most ingenious," Cronco complimented his friend.

"Yes, well, I guess I should've recalled I have this in my arsenal." Marconi stuffed the dog whistle back in his pocket. He smiled and clapped his friend's metal shoulder. They could have been on stage again performing The Flying Dog act. Even though they were retired from magic, it hadn't left their everyday lives.

CHAPTER 9
The Athens Hotel

I asked Neptune if he was pleased with the story so far and he seemed a little put off. Not angry, we wouldn't want that, but he was curious to know when he was going to appear. I promised him soon, I told him the story was building to it, I knew what I was doing. He shrugged, he said he hoped so, and he told me he had somewhere to be. It was time for Neptunalia when the gods and goddesses and the whole pantheon would celebrate. Since I was taking a break from the book, I asked if I could tag along. How often do you get to follow a god? He said okay. I could go with him as far as The Athens Hotel.

That was fine with me. I left the typewriter and my notes. Being a writer, I'm used to contact with other worlds and their inhabitants. Like ghosts, they get in touch with me, so I do a book for them. You wouldn't believe how many there are, they must be standing in line with their stories. I never worked for a God before, but after Neptune found me, how could I refuse? I put on my coat and got my shoes and sat down next to the window to tie the laces. Neptune was waiting for me. The God of the Roman Empire was a black and white goldfish.

After being a nickel for a while, after telling me who he was, he settled on being in a fishbowl on the bookshelf. Neptune seemed quite ordinary floating about. He made a circle, I wrote a page. He was here to inspire and make sure I do my job. Not that I consider this a job. I have other jobs. I'll be at one of them soon.

I looked out the window and couldn't see a cloud in sight.

The Athens Hotel was four blocks away. It would be a nice walk. I would fit right in with the sunny day, like Atlas carrying a goldfish bowl.

CHAPTER 10
American Automaton

Even when I wasn't writing it, the story was continuing in my imagination. I saw Marconi and Cronco outside the aluminum wall of The American Automaton Artificial Limb & Repairs. Marconi was in a joyous mood—they were finally getting the poor robot a new leg, one meant for him, one that he deserved. No more looking in furniture shops for a cheap replacement, a remnant, a secondhand baluster, or picking through the selection of fenceposts and drainpipes at the hardware store.

That's the way it had been. Marconi making a scene, "I want the best leg of wood for my friend here, the very best you have. Sky's the limit." Mumbling while his eyes roamed, "You know I used to come here too, back when I was in a similar condition, Cronco. I got a very good piece of hemlock for my peg. Look here—I must say this old hickory post seems perfect for the job. Above all, you need comfort. Like these shoes I've got. If I'm not wearing crepe soles, I feel like I'm in one of those dreams where I have sandbags for feet." Inevitably, once he saw the price tag, his tune changed. That's how Cronco ended up hobbled on pine. But that was then, and ever since they had been saving, painting portraits, selling balloons and walking dogs.

Marconi crooned his tune, "This is it! Money is no objection, only the best for you, Cronco!" They were shown to the back of American Automaton where an item was on hold.

I can leave them there for a bit. I'm sure they'll be fine. They'll go in there and look at merchandise and Marconi will be grandiose purchasing their very best robot leg. How happy they'll be when that happens.

I'm at The Athens Hotel. Not inside, Neptune insisted I go to the alley. I never know where Neptunalia will happen. Next thing I know, I'm carrying a goldfish bowl up a fire escape. Yes, it was dangerous. One of the ladder steps had rusted off, it was a stretch getting past. Neptune sloshed around and water spilled down my coat, but I tried to be careful as I could.

When we reached the fourth floor, Neptune stopped me next to the window. It used to be a ballroom. The Fletcher Henderson Orchestra once played there. Red curtains were drawn. I could hear the music and laughter and shouts of Neptunalia in progress. He told me to knock on the glass.

As soon as I did, the curtains parted and a woman pushed the window open. I recognized her. I've seen her before on Railroad Avenue. Once I saw her on the corner of Cornwall very carefully shaking a packet of flower seeds onto the sidewalk as if they stood a chance of growing on concrete. "You got Neptune?" she said.

Neptune stuck his head out of the water and introduced me to Aphrodite.

There was an age long ago when the Mediterranean was blue and magical. Neptune couldn't think of anything else but her. Without her, he sat in a spell in a cave deep underwater. Anytime the currents brought them together—it didn't matter if it was warm blue sandy shallows or the cold jade-colored tides—they would collide.

And when Neptunalia reunited all the immortals, you never knew what would happen. I've taken him a few times and each time there would be mayhem, elation, long-standing jealousies, fights, rapture, I don't know what else. Being only mortal, the fire escape is as close as I get.

"Hello," I said to her.

Neither one of these gods looked the way they do in paintings.

She held out her hands. Neptune told me to come back for him tonight. I reminded him I have to work. He said, fine, fine, afterwards then. They are not victims of time the way we are. So I gave Aphrodite the goldfish bowl. For a moment she almost dropped it, or maybe she pretended to. Anyway, I got more water on my sleeve. She cackled and took him behind the curtains and shut the window again.

I was left to go back the way I had come.

As I walked, I thought of Marconi and Cronco and they reappeared. They were ready for adventure.

There was a new spring in Cronco's step. A new spring in a new leg from another #501 model. The leg fit perfectly. As much as he could, Cronco tried to be Gene Kelly, taking hold of a lamppost and swinging around. It was easy going in circles, easy with two left legs. When he was dizzy, he stopped. A crumpled flyer taped to the pole came off stuck to his claw. He couldn't help but read the big words scrawled on it:

LOST GOLDFISH

CHAPTER 11
Poseidon Fish n Chips

The meaning of those words didn't register for me until later. I forgot about Cronco and Marconi as I got caught up in my own world again. The smoky breeze told me when I arrived.

Poseidon Fish n Chips is an old red English double-decker bus. Parked forever on the corner of 11th Street. They gave me my first job when I moved to this town. They were nice to me at a time I was barely making ends meet. Even after I found my current office job and long after I don't have to work in a bus anymore, I told my boss to call me if they ever need help. I'm just loyal that way. Today I'm covering for the dishwasher who called in sick.

The Bristol Commercial Vehicle company didn't build their vehicle to run fried fish to-and-fro and out the door, but that's how it's been transformed.

The seats in the aisle on the first floor have all been taken out, replaced by shelves and cupboards, boxes and sacks, freezers, a coffee maker, a soda machine, a stovetop, deep friers, all jumbled and stacked together in a long kitchen sardine can. Up there in the driver's seat, a Poseidon mannequin watched me cross the street. Painted eyes, a blue captain's suit and visored cap, plastic hands at rest on the wheel.

Chuck saw me coming too and waved from the window. I saw him pass the other windows as he crossed them to the door in back. A couple tourists sat at the table in the yard. Most of our customers come from out of town somewhere, they are drawn to places like Poseidon's.

Chuck said, "We got a problem with the sink."

Oh, no. The same thing happens a few times a year. The Bristol K5G was not designed with plumbing. Chuck had a friend who knew someone who could do it. If you knew Chuck, you'd know what to expect: he got what he paid for. "The same old trouble?" I asked.

"'Fraid so."

I stepped up on the platform and he passed me a wrench. As I ducked around the doorframe,

I got my first look at the sink. A full gray pool. It looked like two days of dishes surrounded it. There was a stack of coffee cups three feet high.

Chuck read my mind or the look on my face, "We haven't had water for a few days, sorry. I was hoping it would fix itself."

This is what I mean, this is why they need me. I said, "You have to call a good plumber and get the whole thing redone."

"I will," Chuck said, "When I have a million dollars, right?" He laughed and when he did it's like that song, the whole world laughs with you. I reached under the sink and turned the valve off. I would need to go outside and get the bucket and pail. I had this to a science. "Are you the only one working today?"

Chuck nodded, "Just me and my shadow running the show."

I pointed at the window, at the couple standing there, "You've got some business. I need to get my buckets."

"Right," Chuck told me, "Right. Well, good luck."

"Okay." I needed luck. I could have used Marconi's magic, or Cronco's superhuman strength to unlock the drain. It took me an hour to clear it. And then I had all those dishes to wash. I was scratched and scalded, my hands stung, and I was sore all over. I don't know, I think maybe I forgot what it's like to work these jobs. The stress of an office gets to me too, but I'm not so weary I can't write. That's the work I'm here for. Even if nobody but Neptune knows it. Over the years I've been telling myself it doesn't matter if anyone else sees my books. I print them at the photocopy shop and I leave them in a row on the shelf at the Eastlake Café. That might be as far as they'll go, but that's something, isn't it? And who knows, maybe these books are seen in another reality, I don't know. I pretend that's true. I told Chuck at the end of my shift I was done.

He stared at me. "What?"

"I think maybe it's time I retire."

No more Poseidon Fish n Chips! It took me all these years to finally leave. I had torn my sleeve. My hands stung from the chlorine and hot plates. And I made fifteen dollars for three hours work.

I laughed. Leaving there for the last time left me with a lingering electric charge. For a block I felt like the star of a jukebox, one of those working-class heroes. I could do anything, hop in a hotwired Cadillac and drive anywhere, but first I had to stop by The Athens Hotel and get Neptune.

Back at the alley, I climbed the fire escape to the windows on the fourth floor and found they were all boarded up with old pallet slats nailed together, rusted and worn. It seemed this floor had been abandoned for years. That was strange…It was the right hotel, there was only one Athens. I couldn't understand it. I returned to the cobblestones and turned the corner and went in the lobby.

I like the smoky marble floor. The Athens is one of those hotels that's been allowed to grow elderly, from the cracks on the floor to the ones in the yellowing wallpaper and ceiling. There's a lot of dark wood, an ancient elevator, a potted palm tree and a chandelier that is home to a spider web.

The guy at the counter was reading a paperback.

"Hello," I said.

He held his hand in his book and turned his attention to me. "You want a room?"

"No. I'm confused. I'm looking for someone in the ballroom on the fourth floor."

"There's no such thing."

"What do you mean? I left my friend in there three hours ago. There were lots of people. I climbed up the fire escape and passed him through a window."

"You climbed the fire escape? You're not supposed to do that."

"Can you let me check the room at least? Maybe he's sitting in there."

"I'm telling you. The ballroom hasn't been used for years. That whole floor is condemned."

"Can you just humor me?"

"You want to see an empty floor?"

I persisted. I couldn't leave Neptune without at least trying.

"I'll get a bellhop…" the clerk sighed and muttered, "If that'll make you go away," as if I couldn't hear. He rang a bell on the counter and we waited in mutual silence. The electric charge that propelled me here was long gone, fizzled out. I was distressed. It didn't help when a gorilla appeared from a backroom. This is it, I figured, I'm about to get evicted.

"Pongo," said the Athens clerk, pointing his book at me, "this fellah here wants to see the fourth floor. Will you do him the pleasure?"

The gorilla grunted. I've never seen a white gorilla before, or one wearing a hotel uniform for that matter. He thudded towards the elevator and I followed. He rattled the metal grating aside and we stepped into the small space. The floor shook and slanted his way. He prodded the round 4 button and it activated a series of clanks and rusty screeches as we began to slowly ascend.

I wasn't sure what to say. I kept quiet. I thought about the gorilla's tailor. I noticed he was missing a gold coat button, but I wasn't about to point that out. I watched the light on the numbered panel overhead. The 4 took its time getting bright, flickering like a candle. When we scratched to a halt, Pongo unlatched the iron grill door of our cage and let me look out.

I faced a sign on a silver post that read: NO ACCESS. The red carpet in the hallway floated past locked, taped-over doors, and ended in a blockade in front of the ballroom. The doorway was made impassible by a piano stacked with steamer trunks, a moose head, hat racks and chairs.

I explained my bewilderment, how the room existed only hours ago and how I left my friend in a goldfish bowl, and how I promised I would get him again, but Pongo's expression remained stony, unmoved. I could tell they wanted me to believe the ballroom didn't exist, there was nothing to see behind that door. I knew it wasn't true, but what could I do?

There was no getting through to those eyes, but I bet Pongo could move that piano if he wanted to.

CHAPTER 13
Disappearance

I put up signs. What else do you do when you lose a god?

LOST GOLDFISH
Black and white, in glass bowl
Last seen at Athens Hotel
Reward Offered

Don't ask me what reward I was prepared to offer. Maybe Neptune could grant the power to speak jellyfish. Honestly, I wasn't that worried about losing him forever. Neptune liked to disappear, especially when it rained. When it rained, he could take human form, walk along as an old man leaning on a trident. I think that's why he favors the Pacific Northwest. Nearly all year it rains. I knew he would be okay. Neptune would find water somewhere in town and in his own time find his way back to the City Locks and our house beside it, there against the parking lot, off of Commodore Way.

After all the time it took going to Woolworths to buy paper and pens and tape to make flyers, after tiring a couple blocks putting them on lampposts and windows, I stopped and sat on a bench. I convinced myself all I needed was faith. That's something I have to keep reminding myself of. I'm not alone. I started for home. Neptune would return.

The disappearance of a whole hotel floor shouldn't be a surprise either. The gods wanted it gone, so it was gone.

CHAPTER 14
The Finder of Lost Souls

The next morning the telephone woke me up. I bumped my toe going around the end of the bed, hopping to the next room. When I got to the kitchen clock, I could see it was 6:31. Who calls at this hour? "Hello?"

"Good day," a man said, "I'm calling in regard to the leaflet."

"What?"

"Are you the owner of a purloined fish?"

Oh, God…There's only one person I know who talks like that. I've written five books about him, including this one. As he detailed his adventures and accomplishments, I couldn't believe this was happening. That familiar voice continued, "And I have a mechanical mastermind, a robot of the highest ability who never misses a clue." I already knew I was speaking to Marconi, but I didn't let on. This had to be another aberration like the disappearance at The Athens Hotel.

I said, "That's all very good, Mr. Marconi, but I'm not looking for a detective. Frankly, I'm—" but he interrupted me.

"I'm no gumshoe, sir!"

"Okay," I said, "Sorry."

"You're speaking to one of the great finders of lost souls! No matter how inexplicable!"

"I'm sure of that," I told him. I know he thinks so. I also knew this phone call had gone on long enough. "I'll tell you what…" I said, "If you find my goldfish, let me know. I'm going back to sleep."

CHAPTER 15
Intuition

The Great Marconi settled the telephone back in its cradle.

"What did he say?" Cronco asked.

Marconi raised his chin imperiously and declared, "We're on the case, my friend!" He handed the Lost Goldfish flyer to Cronco.

The robot placed it in his cupboard-like hatch, next to a box of crackers, two tin cans, and a spare sparkplug. "Where would be a good place to begin?"

Marconi laughed, "Why, at the beginning of course! We'll go to The Athens Hotel!" He reached for his top hat and cane. "Do you know what? I feel that this simple sounding plea to find a lost fish could very well become our greatest performance. I can't explain it…" he pressed the worn tuxedo cloth over his heart, "It isn't something I can explain to a rational being such as yourself. There are no numbers, or charts, or blueprints involved. It's my human intuition."

Gears whirred in the metal box atop Cronco's shoulders. Thoughts. It was no mystery. A robot's heart relied on input, answers and preset reactions to situations, feelings registered as dots and dashes on a paper reel. But as time went by, experience added to knowledge, he developed his own responses, based on what he'd witnessed in his metered life on earth. He had spent enough time with Marconi to know that yes, that crumpled flyer carried inside him could very easily be a catalyst. Rhyme or reason didn't matter. He could feel it too.

And yet there was something more to this new endeavor. Cronco's gleaming eyes were fixed on the letter pushed under the door, no doubt from the landlord. The start of every month was a dance for rent due. "Did our employer confirm a payment wage?"

"Matters of monetary recompense were not discussed," Marconi puffed. "I'm sure we'll be rewarded handsomely upon delivery." He paused at the door and turned the handle.

Cronco pointed a claw at Marconi's worn leather shoe. "You are standing upon a rent notice, I believe."

"Ohhhhh…" Marconi wheezed as he bent to retrieve it. "Is there no end to our persecution?" But as he turned the envelope over, he squinted at the fine print and said, "No…it's not…it's from the Department of Internal Revenue." His demeanor transformed, "Ahah! This is no humbug! I know what this is! Our tax return! Every year I claim you as a robot dependent, we get a $200 refund. This is a sign! You see, this repays your leg expenditure! The universe has compensated us. We'll go to the bank when we get a chance. Here, kindly put this in your vault."

"I am not a mailbox, you know."

"Please Cronco—just for safekeeping."

"I am not a safe either."

Marconi shut his eyes. Was it true his old mechanical friend was becoming more crusty with age? Perhaps. Perhaps they both were. He calmly explained, "I don't mean to imply any such thing. I merely hope that you would do me a favor."

Grudgingly, Cronco accepted the letter and dropped it next to the goldfish flyer and the crackers, two tin cans and the spare sparkplug. Unsaid words stuck in the relays.

Outside of The Athens Hotel, Cronco was drawing a portrait of the Baroness Pannonia. She was a regular subject. She sat regally on the bench next to the bus stop sign. He had until the #305 arrived to finish her picture. He made a blue chalk sky around her.

The Great Marconi staggered out of the shade under the canvas hotel awning and headed towards them. His hands were clenched, he held the cane like a scabbard. His voice bellowed ahead of him, "I've never been treated with such impudence!"

Cronco was erasing the jagged charcoal mark that appeared with Marconi's sudden arrival. The baroness rolled her eyes. She knew about the second-rate magician. She couldn't believe Cronco was saddled to their act. More than once, she told the robot he was the one who deserved to be called Great.

Marconi seethed, "I asked about the fourth floor and the clerk had a gorilla toss me out the front door!" Marconi had to catch his breath. He looked from the robot to his art subject. "Are you doing parlor pictures again?"

"I enjoy it," Cronco said.

"You've got a million-dollar gift," the Baroness told Cronco and then she told Marconi, "I doubt you're aware of it, but we're looking at the next Picasso. I have offered him my patronage."

Cronco replied, "I would gladly accept your offer, however I am currently engaged in another job."

Marconi was flabbergasted. "That's right, you are! We're looking for a lost goldfish!"

The Baroness laughed. Then she covered her mouth with her glove. Was Marconi serious?

Cronco sighed. "It is true. I have no genuine desire to follow this endeavor, but I am entitled to accompany my accomplice. I am a robot. Different rules apply to us. Our orders come first. Art comes second."

The appearance of the bus surprised all of them. Cronco hurried to sign his name, the

Baroness hopped to her toes and waved at the driver, while Marconi stood next to them, caught trying to think of what to say. Had he ever been speechless before?

The door hissed open. Cronco passed her the portrait and Pannonia took a step on and turned and reached into her overcoat. "Take my card," she told Cronco. "You must do more work for me."

Cronco put it in his compartment, next to the letter, the lost fish flyer, the cracker, two tin cans and the spare sparkplug.

CHAPTER 17
The End of Neptunalia

Coach Wooden had the radio on every time he drove. He would listen to any sport. One very early morning when the atmospheric conditions were rare, he caught the transmission from a cricket game on the other side of the world. He couldn't understand the rules or the point of the game. It was a game, that's what mattered. The roar of a crowd and the announcer. It could have been the Martian World Series. Coach Wooden let the radio's disembodied voice guide him. That's why he wasn't surprised when he turned the key and started the truck and someone started talking to him in the dead of night. It wasn't the radio though. The voice was coming from where the jingling bottles filled the back of the truck.

He turned around, "What's that?"

The voice repeated, "I said are you going to the

aqueduct?"

The coach squinted at the dark rearview mirror. Nobody was back there. "Who's squawking?"

"My name is Neptune."

"What! Neptune?" the old man slowed. "Did you say *Neptune*?"

"That's right. I'm in here. I'm everywhere."

The coach hit the brakes. Bottles shook and dinned in the lurch. He jumped out the driver's side and scuttled around the truck. A few of the bottles rolled across the floor towards the cab.

Neptune heard the coach scrabbling at the doorlatch. He knew there was going to be trouble. He was just trying to hop a ride with the water, to the aqueduct which would carry him to the locks and the little green house on Commodore Way. He was still a god, but he was at the mercy of whatever was coming, just like the rest of the bottles. Neptune didn't have all his powers. That wasn't surprising, he was a lot older, a thousand years had gone by, but he was no ordinary human. He changed his shape. This time he was a dandelion seed in a bottle of Wooden Water.

It had been a long night since the end of Neptunalia. What happened at The Athens Hotel? All the guests at the celebration, everyone was there, friends and enemies, and someone wickedly put something in his water. Suddenly he couldn't see clearly, the world tilted in the glass, he held to the rim, washed in the poison. Where was Aphrodite? He heard her distant laugh, far from the windowsill. Then he was falling. How he landed at last in a bottle in the back of a delivery truck on Corliss Avenue is anyone's guess.

The door whipped open and Coach Wooden scowled at the contents of his truck. All the bottles shivered a high-pitched tone that set dogs barking for blocks. "Neptune!" he yelped. "Neptune water!"

Neptune kept silent. He didn't know what this mortal was capable of. On the coach's gray sweatshirt, swung round his neck was a silver whistle—maybe he could call forth hellhounds, maybe they were on the way. The shore of the dark lake already echoed with them.

The coach's eyes boiled. "Where are you? Speak up!" To be fair, despite his unbound rage Coach Wooden had good reason to be on guard. Wooden Water wasn't the only supplier of water in town. The Neptune Beverage Company had been steadily taking over. Their Neptune Sparkling Waters brand could be found on the same shelves elbowing his product out of the way. Coach Wooden's bottles looked very plain indeed compared to the competitor's green beach glass with silver labels. The Neptune Beverage Company had a factory next to the interstate where every passing car could see the towering green neon trident sign. They had their water trucked in from the mountain peaks. What did the coach have? A natural spring in his backyard. A garage with bottles on pallets and a hose to fill them by. How was Coach Wooden supposed to compete with them? His was just a small operation. He could claim it had health properties, and he could brag of his long winning career with the local highschool team. But the town was growing older too, he wasn't the celebrity he once was, if anything he was just a curiosity. Loyalty wasn't what it used to be.

Coach reached in and dragged a basket of water bottles towards himself. "I heard you! You can't hide from me!" He had been bedeviled by voices before, when it was fourth and down at the other team's home, the taunting invisible jeer of the loudspeakers echoing over the field, rousing the crowd against him. That pressure only made him stronger. No way was the Neptune Water infection going to win. One by one, he poured out each bottle onto the street.

Neptune didn't have long to wait. By then, the coach was going full steam ahead. His arms were like locomotive pistons. Neptune was splashed in with the stream. He tumbled along the curb, pouring into the drain, down into the tunnels leading to the lake.

Green Lake was alright with Neptune. He would be fine spending the night underwater. He was tired. Reaching the end, he tumbled free of the storm drain and swam and sank. A rocking chair waited for him at the bottom of the lake. It slowly creaked like a cradle. Landing between its arms, Neptune only needed a minute or two to fall asleep...goodnight.

CHAPTER 18
Fifty Years

The next dawn Neptune sat on the edge of a float in the middle of the lake. There was a diving board above him. He was in human form, as long as his legs stayed in the water, he could be fish or man, or something halfway in between. The morning fog was thick enough he couldn't be seen from the shore. He was thinking about what to do. Not that he had to do anything if he didn't want to. Somebody at Neptunalia had it in for him. He wondered if it wouldn't be best to lay low for a while. He could sit in that rocking chair sleeping for the next fifty years and time would slip away like a dream. Then he could come back and see if anyone remembered.

CHAPTER 19
In the Morning

I didn't have any trouble falling asleep after my phone call with Marconi. It was just a dream within other dreams. A vaguely recalled story was forming—the fates of Cronco and Marconi and Neptune were woven together…

When I left the dream, I left a theater, and the story ran on like a movie without me. Past the curtains, my opened eyes looked at all that happened while I was asleep—the sun was shining through a break in the clouds, the fog was moving on Commodore Way, fishing boats came and went, none of it needed my attention.

I had been gone, now I was back.

I really wasn't worried about Neptune. He'll be fine. In this weather he can fit in with the drops of rain. He can make his way home with the early morning fog, brushing across parked cars' dew.

I felt the bed next to me, reaching for my wife. I still do that. I lifted my head and looked at the clock. 8:37. I slept in! It wasn't so early after all. A crow called on the cedar outside our window.

What brings a Roman god coming back here? He wants his story written, I know. I'd also like to believe it's the company, the enjoyment of being part of a family. I'm used to having Neptune around, inspiring me, and when he's not here I'm thinking about him, missing him. As long as I keep writing about him, he'll stick around. If that's all that matters, when I'm done with this book, I guess Neptune will leave.

I hope not.

So even though I tell myself I'm not concerned about him, I was thinking about Neptune when the phone began to ring downstairs. I held my breath, listening to it become hysteric. It wouldn't stop. Someone *had* to talk to me, it was important. I laughed. I supposed it was Neptune, hoping for a ride. He was probably stuck in the buffet aquarium again. I remember the time that happened—a girl tapped the glass and laughed like Dorothy in *The Wizard of Oz*. He got a real joy from making her laugh, you could tell.

It wasn't him though, there was another voice in my ear.

"Oh no," I interrupted, "I told you yesterday, Chuck, I'm not working there anymore...I understand...I'm sorry your dishwasher is still out, I...No, that doesn't interest me...No thank you...No, I don't want to be a part owner of Poseidon Fish n Chips..." It took me five minutes to convince my old boss I meant what I said. I wasn't going back to Poseidon and I meant it.

I leaned down and set the phone back on the table.

While I was thinking about making coffee, the phone rang again. I was popular today.

"Oh God," I groused to myself, "I'm not here, I joined the Navy."

I took a deep breath, enough to swim the Atlantic underwater, and answered the phone. To my surprise, this time it was Neptune. He told me what happened at the Neptunalia. There were gods and goddesses with nothing better to do than act crazy, poison him and throw him out the window. Things often got out of hand. They played games I couldn't understand. One time he got trapped in a watercolor painting. He waited two months on the Goodwill wall. He was on sale for three dollars, down from ten, when he finally sold and was carried out into the freedom of rain.

Sipping at my coffee, I leaned back and listened to his latest story, how he went from water to water, until Coach Wooden appeared. Neptune knew the little blue truck was on its rounds. He figured he could hitch a ride to the aqueduct, hop out at our neighborhood and wait for me to walk past. He told me his plan didn't quite work out that way, but he did make it to a phonebooth on Commodore and 33rd. The dew was still wet on the dial, that's how he made the call. He would be waiting for me in the puddle outside. I knew the corner, I could picture the puddle, it was a good thing he phoned when he did. It was starting to look like sun was on the way and puddles don't last long without rain.

But I figured I had time for one more cup of coffee.

83

CHAPTER 20
Contacting Other Worlds

Neptune never got the chance to swing himself out of the phonebooth into the puddle. A red car stopped at the curb and a woman entered the phonebooth. She picked up the phone and Neptune who was a raindrop landed on her jacket. He watched her get a quarter and drop it in the slot. He didn't have to use coins the way we do—he had power over telephones.

She said, "It's me—June. I'm on my way. See you soon."

Neptune could have taken a chance and leaped from her, bounced from raindrop to raindrop like musical notes, but it was risky, if they stopped, he'd have to find a safe spot to land on the asphalt. He preferred taking chances on her raincoat.

She returned to her open car door. She knew she wouldn't be long in the phonebooth. She hopped behind the wheel and put the car into gear.

When Neptune saw who was sitting next to her, and the couple in the backseat, he laughed. He knew them, he saw them perform on the Neptune Theatre stage way back in 1979.

Neptune was in a chariot full of showbusiness royalty.

Driving the car, cloaked in the black rain jacket, was television star, June Watts. Next to her was her comrade, Rabbit Ears. And in the back seat he recognized the fellows from his book, Marconi and Cronco. It couldn't have been easy getting the robot to sardine himself in.

June drove them away from Commodore Avenue. If Neptune had been looking out the window, he might have seen the author of his book coming to meet him, but he was too entranced by his newfound company. He listened with great interest to their conversation and was able to piece together where they were going.

"Do you really think he can contact a goldfish?" Marconi said.

Rabbit Ears said, "You bet he can! And plenty more besides."

"Even if he can't, it's worth a try," June said. She was always cheerful. On her TV show she would sing and dance with puppets. Marconi gave her a smile. He was pleased he asked June for help, she made him feel better right away. She had that effect.

What a stroke of good luck they all happened to meet on the street. It seemed meant to be. They were each going to find what they needed.

A few minutes later, the car arrived at an ordinary house. You wouldn't see writing that announced:

Feldspar Spoon
Occult Wizard

Instead of that, the sign on the front lawn read:

SANTY'S UPHOLSTERY

And under that in red lettering:

Parking in Back

People like Feldspar Spoon weren't in the phonebook, but there were fortunetellers and seers hidden all over the city. Spoon had a repair business in the garage, fixing car seats and vinyl chairs. Meanwhile, in his house, he had a darkened room for contacting other worlds.

June parked next to an old sedan and they all opened doors. Marconi and Rabbit Ears had to help Cronco get out, pulling on his metal arms. June stared at the lot full of cars, spread around them like a deck of cards. She looked like she was about to start a song or maybe a dance. Neptune hoped not, he could barely cling to the slick fabric of June's coat. He needed a new environment and a different body than a raindrop. Once he had inhabited a pair of false-teeth soaking in a glass of water. That wasn't ideal either...

June turned her song into a hum and led everyone across the gravel to the office door. She knocked and her companions gathered behind her.

A man wearing overalls opened the door and stood there. He chewed a cigar.

June put a finger to her mouth and uttered, "We're here to see Mr. Spoon. We have an appointment, he's expecting us."

When he was done evaluating them—a woman in bright patchwork clothes, a large rabbit, an old magician, a seven-foot-tall robot—he nodded and said, "Go around the corner, try the front door of the house."

CHAPTER 21
Issues

The same man answered her knock at the front door. This time the overalls were gone and he wore a black three-piece suit instead. He had also grown a thin moustache. "May I help you?"

June smiled, "We have an appointment with Mr. Spoon."

"Thank you, madam," he said, "we've been expecting your arrival." They were shown into the waiting room and told, "It will just be a moment please."

Rabbit Ears and Marconi found seats, Cronco stood by a potted fern pedestal, and June moved around the room placidly. She was used to being on sets. This one was a 20th century room, simply furnished with a couch and some chairs, a table holding a stack of magazines. It was the walls that were impressive, they surrounded the visitors with paintings, patched all over, windows to other worlds. June didn't know where to begin.

Neptune stared enviously at the fish tank on the other wall. It was filled with bubbling water… As soon as he could, he would guide June over to it. He coughed dryly, close to her ear.

Rabbit Ears asked, "Do we have any snacks?"

"I'm afraid not," June answered. "This isn't our studio, there's no caterer."

Rabbit Ears sighed.

Cronco opened the latch on his chest compartment. "I brought crackers."

"Crackers?" the giant rabbit bounced to his feet.

June found herself next to the aquarium, staring at the swimming colors. Round and round they went, every fish was a crayon, going somewhere else and returning and leaving again. She found herself humming, listening to the burbling water, shutting her eyes.

Nobody saw the little splash.

A new goldfish materialized in the tank and hid behind a castle.

Marconi should have investigated the aquarium, but he was lost in a copy of *Variety*, searching for mention of his name. Brow creased, he intently turned another page. Nearby, Cronco was sharing crackers with the rabbit.

Deep in a hum, June was remembering her dog who passed on. If it wasn't for Mr. Spoon, she wouldn't have known what happened to her beloved pet. Spoon showed her a miracle. He reached out into the beyond to draw the dog into this reality again. Their reunion only lasted long enough for her to know everything was okay, she could see her dog was living in a beautiful place. She even got to ruffle that dog's soft fur and hold him tight before the sensation and vision faded out.

Marconi picked a copy of *Billboard* off the coffee table and began another fruitless search for himself when a door burst open and a snow-white gorilla lumbered through the doorway. Pongo was no stranger to Marconi, it was the very same ape that tossed the old man from The Athens Hotel just an hour ago. Fearing another assault, Marconi quickly lifted the magazine higher to hide his face.

Pongo didn't seem to register the crowd in the room. He dabbed his eyes with a handkerchief, sniffed, and returned the cotton square to his hotel uniform pocket. His breath came ragged and weighty as an old boiler. He stomped across the floor, wrenched open the daylight and was gone. The whole wall shook, rippled like a pond when a stone falls in.

"My goodness," June said. "That poor creature."

"You're telling me…" came a voice from the open doorway behind her. "That ape's got issues." It was Feldspar Spoon.

CHAPTER 22
The Counterfeit Reality Machine

They were all surprised, even Neptune, by the appearance of the wiry, bent elderly man who greeted them and told them about White Pongo. "Imagine…born in the jungle, shunned by his society because of his color, forced to make do on his own, wrestling beasts, victimized by all the everyday dangers of survival. Then it happens! His world changes. Explorers appear and with them is a beautiful woman." Feldspar Spoon shook his head. "Pamela…That's her name. You should hear him go on about Pamela…Anyway, they shot him, caught him, caged and dragged him by ship to the western world. What did civilization give him? Circuses, sideshows, humiliation, and mindless, menial labor in America. Can you believe it, all that and he still dreams of Pamela? He can't get her out of his heart, he comes here just so he can see her."

Eyes wide, Rabbit Ears asked, "Where is she?" in a hushed voice.

"She's dead," Spoon said. "She died in Santa Monica in 1999."

June gasped. "The love of his life!"

"Yes," Spoon nodded. "I give my clients entrance to a world where there is no dying, only life."

"Séance?" Marconi asked. An old magic man like Marconi had seen the dead appear as shadows on walls and flickering lights.

"No, no, nothing like that. I'm no parlor charlatan," Spoon puffed. "I'll show you. Follow me." The doorway led into a hallway where more paintings clung to the walls like moths. Feldspar Spoon walked slow enough that they could glance into the frames rolling past like apartment windows on the street.

Rabbit Ears said, "I sure do like your paintings. They're neat."

Spoon smiled, "I'm just an old man, all I will leave behind are my paintings. I've seen the future. When these are discovered, they will be my gift to the world. My only legacy. My Counterfeit Reality machine will be destroyed. There will be no way for anyone to go back and forth in time, for good or bad."

Marconi repeated, "Counterfeit Reality Machine?" What a marvelous name, what an illusion that must be.

Spoon paused at the bolted door they had come to. "Time is not so difficult to bend. We do it all the time with memories and dreams. But being able to participate in otherworldly times required the invention of a machine. Let's have a look at it, shall we?" He leaned on the door like a white-haired dandelion and pushed.

It must have been a child's room at one time, there were nursery scenes painted on the wall, storks and castles, wooded hills where dragons lived. Maybe there was a Spoon family living in this house long ago. In the center of the room where there might have been a crib long ago, rested a film projector pointed at a blank movie screen stand.

"Golly," said Rabbit Ears, "Is that the time machine?"

"It's much more than that. It creates an open dimension to another reality, overlapped with ours."

"Oh," said Rabbit Ears.

"It's a wonderful machine!" June attested, "It let me be with my dog again. I could see that she was okay. She's happy in another world. I don't know how you found her, Mr. Spoon."

"Animals have a strong presence and connection with the people who love them. Even after they're gone, they shine like a light in the dark. After dying, people don't generally stick around, they travel on, but animals are loyal. They wait for you. That power can be keyed into. I find them with the Counterfeit Reality Machine. This is why people come to me, this is what I'm known for…That and my upholstery business on the other side." He pointed at the faded Mother Hubbard painted on the wall shared with the garage. "There is nothing lost in the past, or in this world of ours, or in the next one to come. I can find who you're looking for, wherever they are."

Marconi was impressed. He elbowed his silent robot companion and whispered hoarsely, "What do you think of that?"

Long ago it was decided machines could do anything. Cronco observed the Counterfeit Reality contraption silently, with red unblinking eyes.

Spoon regarded June and asked her, "Who are your friends seeking to find?"

She turned to Marconi who took a breath and grandly answered Feldspar Spoon, "We're looking for a lost goldfish."

CHAPTER 23
Nick the Eel vs. The Tin Terror

The inventor of Counterfeit Reality had rediscovered all species of dearly departed animals—there was no reason a goldfish, living or not, wouldn't register in his machine—but he didn't get a chance to try. Someone else had entered the room behind them, someone with shoes that creaked the floorboards.

The footsteps stopped next to Marconi and a gravelly voice announced, "You doing business with fishmongers now, Spoon?"

Feldspar Spoon, so erudite a moment ago sputtered, "Oh, Mr. Eel! I wasn't expecting you. I was just, I—"

"Tut, tut," hushed Nick the Eel, as he was known in the underworld. He patted Cronco's shoulder, "Who's the tin terror?"

Spoon stumbled over words, "Er—these are—I was just showing my visitors around."

"Yeah okay, well show-and-tell is over. Everybody scram." Nick poked a thumb at the door. "Except for you, professor." In his hand he held a black heavy-looking bag like the one William Carlos Williams would carry in the snow.

Nobody wanted to leave him alone with a gangster, but Spoon shooed his guests away as if they were mayflies. They all agreed he was in danger though. June took Rabbit Ears' big paw and pulled him towards the door, with Marconi bustling close behind. Marconi muttered, "No wonder this happened—you're just asking for the criminal element when you name your invention a Counterfeit Reality machine. It sounds like a gangster's science fiction dream."

While Cronco wheezed after them, he cautiously opened his compartment and removed a tin can, leaving it on a shelf next to the Dr. Seuss book, *McElligot's Pool.* Cronco was no fool. He shut the bolted nursery door with a claw and tuned the radio signal in his head.

CHAPTER 24
A John Dillinger Movie

The Counterfeit Reality machine whirred and spread a blurry scene on the movie screen. Feldspar Spoon focused it and sharpened the image to crystal clarity. A room formed. It was a bank vault room, white tiled floor, where the walls on either side were layers of drawers and deposit boxes. The far wall was dominated by a round safe door.

Nick the Eel was pleased. His plan was working, all his hard work was going to pay off. He was almost giddy as he explained to Spoon how he bought a mouse from Lucky Pete's Pet Shop and spent two weeks feeding it gorgonzola, provolone and other delicacies until the mouse would run to him and curl on his hand. It was love. Brainwashing was so easy, Nick told Spoon. Calypso the mouse was devoted to him. Yesterday, he put Calypso in an empty cardboard box of Blammos, bedded with cotton cloth, with a sleeping pill wrapped inside Swiss. Just before the Key Bank closed, he had the teller deposit the cigar box in the vault.

Calypso slept dead to the world and dreamed of Nick the Eel.

Nick pointed at the glowing drawer on the wall, "That's where Calypso is!" The bond between them was strong enough that the Counterfeit Reality machine had no trouble finding her.

Nick the Eel raised his arm, "I brought along a little merchandise for the job." He unzippered the black bag…the pause was imminent poetry, as he reached in, grabbed the dynamite sticks, pushed around Spoon and stepped right into the projected beam of light.

It was like watching a John Dillinger movie. Eel was quick—he had to be—you never knew exactly how long it would last—he didn't want to be marooned in a bank with the vault about to blow up. Only Houdini could get out of that. He placed the explosives and lit the fuses and ran across the tiles back into Spoon's nursery.

"How's that, professor?" He grinned and waited for the bang.

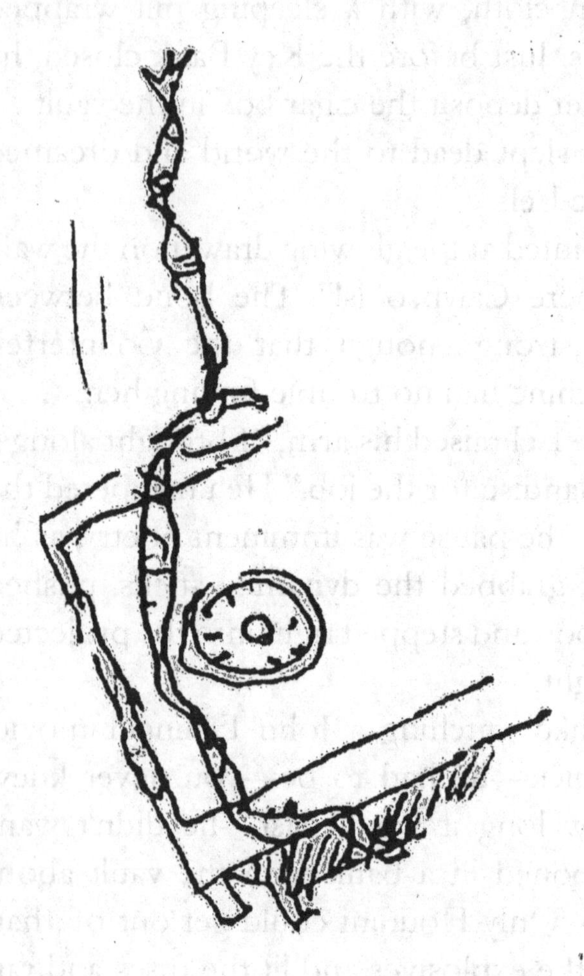

CHAPTER 25
Only in Tokyo

Even though they were separated by another reality, the house shook. Nick the Eel tied a red handkerchief around his face and leaped back into the screen, into the bank smoke and dust. Alarm bells clamored as he crunched over the debris, past the broken safe door towards all that money that awaited him.

While this was happening, back in Spoon's house, down the hall, past the paintings, into the waiting room and outside, down the path to the street, on the sidewalk, June, Rabbit Ears and Marconi were gathered around Cronco. He held a talking tin can in his claw. The second can, the one he left on the nursery shelf, was the other end of his tin can telephone. They heard every word being said in the nursery, it was like listening to *Gang Busters* on the radio. They could picture

Nick the Eel stuffing a gunnysack full of hundred-dollar bills. A distant wail of police sirens whined downtown.

"What should we do?" Rabbit Ears asked.

"I knew that hoodlum was no good!" Marconi seethed.

June said, "We need to go back inside and help poor Mr. Spoon."

Feldspar Spoon wasn't quite as helpless as they assumed. Every once in a while, an experiment reaches an unaccountable end. A beaker needs to be emptied down the drain, a faulty invention disassembled back into parts, a blackboard erased of words, papers crumpled and thrown away, a counterfeit reality never to be seen again. My God, Spoon thought, where will it end with Nick the Eel? Is this just the beginning of his crime wave? After his success with Calypso, what was next? Will he befriend a bee in a jewelry store window? Will he look for a parakeet on the *Titanic* to bond with and go through time to rob what he can before the ship sinks? Spoon was sure that someone like Eel would never be satisfied…as soon as he returns from the bank he'll want more.

Spoon turned the projector off.

The image of the bank vault disappeared. All the noise became quiet.

The nursery was a peaceful room, with a square of sunlight on the floor and Peter Rabbit on the wall with a carrot in his paws.

June Watts tapped on the door and warily pushed it open. "Mr. Spoon? Are you okay?"

Spoon held onto the Counterfeit Reality machine with both hands. It was warm, almost hot, but he didn't let go. "I've never done that before," he said. "I've never left someone stranded, but I had no choice. I had to. This machine must not be used unlawfully."

"Of course not, Mr. Spoon," June soothed.

"It never crossed my mind to use it that way. What a devious thing to do."

"We know," June said. Rabbit Ears set a paw on the inventor's shoulder.

"Don't be disheartened," Marconi piped up. "I once had a sailor go AWOL inside my transmigration cabinet. Two days later he staggered out in Topeka."

Spoon insisted, "All I wanted to do was help people find their animals. I'm afraid I've been foolish, I let myself be used."

"Cheer up," Rabbit Ears said.

"That's right, Mr. Spoon." June Watts was always reminding the children watching her show that they were more than the obstacles put in their way. Then she cried, "Oh dear!" taking a pocket watch from her coat, "The time! We've got a television show to do!"

Rabbit Ears quickly regarded his comical wristwatch. The hour hand swung and stuck. Maybe only in Tokyo was it telling the right time.

June's eyes shone, "Do you think—would you all like to come to the studio with us?"

"Say!" Rabbit Ears clapped his paws. "What a great idea! We can have special guests today!"

"Yes, you're all so wonderful," June continued, "Marconi—you and Cronco could do some of your magic—and Mr. Spoon, can you tell the children about animals and how their love never goes away? Oh, won't this be fun!"

"I have nothing on my agenda," Marconi stated. "Cronco?" The robot remained mute, unreadable, he was only half paying attention to the world around him. Inside his shell he had the radio on. Marconi grinned, "It would be our pleasure to comply."

June turned to the quiet inventor, "What do you say, Mr. Spoon?"

He pulled his hands off the machine. It was cooling. "I suppose…There's nothing more I can do here…but I do wish I knew what's happening at the bank."

Cronco, who had been listening to the airwaves all this time, reported, "They caught him. I heard it on the police channel."

"What about the mouse?" Spoon asked Cronco. "Did they find Calypso?"

"I am not sure at this time. There has been no mention of a mouse."

Marconi chuckled, "But it will make a fine ending for the story when they do."

CHAPTER 26
The Nearest Rain

The KGUS radio and television building is on a diamond shaped block where Liberty and Ellis streets meet. A tall antenna emits messages to the sky. In the lot, June Watts has her star on a sign where she parked her car. Anyone who grew up in the Pacific Northwest thought of her that way: a star. Anyone, that is, who grew up with a TV on in the early evening, when the sunset gleams the telephone wires and the crows are heading for their roosts.

The studio was busy with final preparations, lighting, sound, the movement of cameras. June Watts had her usual spot to get made up. There wasn't much she needed to become her TV character. Most of her stayed that way all the time, they just needed to add a little paint.

Her cohost Rabbit Ears was also easy to

prepare, a six-foot rabbit only had to walk on the set. He kept out of the way, over by the end of the cardboard garden wall.

A familiar man was talking to him. Half in the shadows, he seemed delighted to be talking with the rabbit. He shook the rabbit's paw and was genuinely delighted.

"Rabbit Ears!" someone with a clipboard yelled, "Two minutes!"

Marconi intercepted as the big rabbit passed. "When do we go on? I just ask in order to prepare myself. I prefer to wear a cape in my act. Is there one I can borrow?"

"Ummm—"

"And if you don't mind me asking, who were you talking to just now?"

"He said his name was James Stewart."

"That's what I thought," Marconi beamed.

"He asked me if I know Harvey."

"Do you?"

"Of course I do!" And with that, Rabbit Ears was on his way. He was ready to laugh and sing and make believe. A moth chased after him.

"Did you hear that?" Marconi asked Cronco. "I wonder if Mr. Stewart is here for the program.

Do you think he's going to be another guest? You know I've always wanted to meet him. How about you, Feldspar? Are you a fan?"

"I'm sorry. I haven't been listening. I'm still worried about that mouse."

"Oh, well my friend here is a walking, talking radio. Any news yet, Cronco?"

Cronco searched the wavelengths, picking through them like a motorboat in shallow tidal waters, finding the right channel on the VHF spectrum. He listened intently and gave their report, "The nearest rain is twenty-one miles away."

CHAPTER 27
June on the Moon

I miss going to the movies. I miss the Neptune Theatre's calendar I would magnet onto the refrigerator. I miss that feeling as the sun is going down and night is falling, and the lights of the city are on and there's a double feature starting in an hour. I know they've gone the way of the unicorn and harpsichords. Now I make do with June Watts. I still like to watch her show every night before dinner, it takes me to a happy childhood world where imagination is everything. I may be in the kitchen, making spaghetti, but I listen, and as soon as I can I'm there on the couch with my television family.

After *June on the Moon*, I'll do the dishes. Then I'll do some writing or read or watch a movie. I'll go to bed and before falling asleep, I always wonder about the billboard on Lincoln Street. It's another

Feldspar Spoon invention. One we're all aware of, I should say. This one uses special receivers on the radio tower to search the town for dreams. Our dreams hover in layers and the machinery fishes through them until it nets one and carries it through the night air to where it will shine on the billboard like the dearly departed Sunset Drive-In screen. I always wonder if it will be my turn. It has to happen sooner or later.

Tonight, I was already eating when June's show came on.

Everything seemed fine until a six-foot rabbit walked on stage with a robot. I was fine with the rabbit, I was used to him, and I guess I was used to the robot too, but seeing Cronco on the reality of TV was shocking. He was exactly the way I picture him when I write books. Even the dents were authentic. And I knew if he opened that compartment I would see Pannonia's personal card, the goldfish flyer, the crackers, two tin cans, the spare sparkplug and the letter from the Department of Internal Revenue. I have a vivid imagination that was becoming true.

I stood up before Marconi appeared, as I felt sure he would, and went to the kitchen. Did they know I'd be watching? What am I supposed to make of my fictional characters becoming real? I suppose it's not so different than Neptune wanting to be real on paper, they're just doing it the other way around, going from the page into actuality.

I ran water in a pan.

I was full of questions.

I knew their story, I knew what they had been through and what took them to the television studio, but I didn't know why they became *real*, or what would happen next. Was I still in control of them? Was I ever? I don't know if I created them and gave them life, or if they've had that power all along. I don't know if I'm writing the stories and making them happen, or writing what already exists somewhere else, in another world I'm merely reporting on. From real life to writing, I go back and forth like the tide.

And now they're here, washed ashore.

Look what happens when I let them alone! What have they gone and done? Would I be able to go to my typewriter and reign them back in? Somehow they have stepped through the same way the Counterfeit Reality machine propels to another world. Are they even on paper anymore, are they free, if I look at the manuscript will there be blank white clouds on it? I put my hands in the warm soapy water and held a spoon. I knew who to ask these questions. I hoped Feldspar Spoon might have answers for me.

CHAPTER 28
The Fake

"Do you know," Marconi confessed, "I enjoyed our time on television. I've got a notion to accept June's offer and be a regular on her show! Imagine that, Cronco. A regular gig! No more menial toil. I can stick to my heart's calling—magic!" He sighed and chuckled, "I admit I'm getting starry-eyed." He paused for a dramatic moment before they left the studio, half-wanting to run back down the hall. Then he resumed, "But it hasn't helped our chances of finding the goldish." He held the door open for Cronco and they went onto the sidewalk, into the lights of passing cars. "I guess we'll just go home and leave it at that. A failed enterprise."

"On the contrary," Cronco replied, "It was most fortuitus that we met June Watts. I believe she led us directly to that fish."

Marconi halted. "What?"

"At the Feldspar Spoon house, as we entered the waiting room, there were seven fish in the tank. When we left the room there were eight."

Marconi gaped. "Was it—?"

"A black and white one."

"But how could that happen? What can it mean?"

"I am not able to process that yet."

Marconi shook his head, "I'm flabbergasted! I really am."

"Yes," Cronco agreed, "It is perplexing."

They weren't far from their apartment, a few more blocks. The electric glow of the broadcasting station shined on Cronco's metal back.

A car parked by the curb stirred. The door opened and a sequined suit emerged. The man wearing it looked vaguely familiar. "Excuse me!" he hailed them. "I saw you leave the premises. I assume you're fellow entertainers? Let me guess…" He scratched his chin thoughtfully with a ring-covered hand, "You're producers, aren't you?"

There's an unwritten rule that those in show biz stick together. Marconi allowed the man to make his plea. Marconi may have been a second fiddle magician in a threadbare tuxedo, but he didn't mind being mistaken for one of the elites. He nodded and listened.

"I do a little tribute act out on Lake City Way. I do alright, I've got regulars. They like me, I've got talent. I'm an impersonator, but I'm much more. I pay a commendable service to a legend in the field. I got a writeup in *The Shopper's Gazette* that says so. I'm believable but I'm not in the position to really step into his shoes. Not yet. I can't actually *be* the great Sylvan Moore, can I? Or can I? It's not like I'm going to bump him off and take his place. I mean, I think I could, I feel confident I could, I have the looks and capacity, but I need someone truly familiar with Sylvan Moore to be on the level with me. That's all I want from you. Can you come see the show? It would mean a lot to get an insider's opinion."

Marconi tried, "We appreciate your offer, but I'm afraid my associate and I are enroute to a previous engagement, one we can't possibly delay any longer." Marconi didn't want to say it, but the man bore only the feeblest resemblance to the renowned Sylvan Moore. Like a penny with a poor profile.

"Just do me the favor of seeing my show. Please."

Marconi glanced at Cronco. Maybe it was time for a robot to intervene.

"Alright, that's it!" The fake Sylvan Moore grunted as he reached through the open window of his car and pulled out a disintegrator pistol. "I tried to be polite with you guys. I work hard for years and I get no further than the Tiki Hut on Lake City Way! Now I'm going to *insist* you two are coming with me and you're going to see my show 'Mel is Moore' and I'm going to get what I want. Get in the car!"

TV

CHAPTER 29
A Nite with Melvin Shore

"Ladies and gentlemen, here he is again! Put your hands together for Melvin Shore!" As the music flared, a waitress walked directly in front of him, blocking the view of him as he bounded to the stage. She carried a tray full of drinks and prawns. He stopped at the microphone stand as she continued on to the tables. He peered into the spotlight and tapped the microphone.

"Thank you very much!" he said. "Thank you." There was a lot of noise in the Tiki Room, a lot of laughter and talking, not much applause, especially now that he stood there, holding the mic like a shoe salesman. "It's good to be back. Say, did you read the *Herald* today? Did you see the weather report? Where's the rain, guys? Am I right? I don't know about you, but I carried an umbrella all day long for nothing. Finally, Mary Poppins wanted it back." His act didn't get any better. Neither was his singing an improvement. When he introduced Marconi and Cronco at stage side, they were the only ones paying attention to him—Marconi wishing he had mastered invisibility, Cronco thinking how fine it would be to be a lonely buoy on the lake—both of them keenly aware of the ray-gun Melvin had tucked into his sparkling suit coat. At the end of fifteen long minutes, he thanked the room and reminded everyone, "Be sure to pick up a copy of my album at the door." He waved an L.P, *A Nite with Melvin Shore.* "You've been a privilege and a pleasure, see you for the second show if you're lucky." He departed his stage podium leaving the fake palm tree rocking slightly and headed for his two guests.

Marconi held a rigid smile, Cronco betrayed no emotion, phony or otherwise.

"What did you guys think?" Melvin panted.

Marconi cupped his ear, "What's that?" hoping the noise in the room might give him a little time to come up with something.

Melvin lit a cigarette and exhaled, "Come along with me. Let's find somewhere we can talk."

The Tiki Hut cooler was about as quiet as you could get, just a steady rumble of the condenser motors and the fans spreading cold air.

Marconi was out of compliments and close to pleading, "Like I said earlier, Mr. Shore. As much as we've enjoyed the evening, we have an important assignment we must attend to. You needn't drive us there, we can call for a taxi."

"What could be more important than this?" Melvin puffed a cold cloud.

"We are investigating a lost goldfish," Cronco informed him.

"What?"

"A black and white goldfish," Cronco steamed.

"Are you kidding me? So what? What can a goldfish do that I can't?"

"Several things," Cronco elucidated, "beginning

with breathing underwater. Then there is the ability to—"

Melvin cut him off, "Okay, enough!"

The cooler door opened as a waitress stuck her head in, "Mr. Shore, we need you for your second show."

"Already? It's only been ten minutes."

"I know," she replied, "The ventriloquist canceled."

Melvin groaned. "Well, you know what they say—the show must go on! Let's go fellahs…"

Marconi rubbed his hands together, "I'll be glad at least to get out of this cooler."

"One moment," Cronco rasped. "My feet have frozen to the floor."

Melvin paused in the open doorway, "Are you joking?"

Cronco said, "If we were joking, it would be the first one all night."

"Hey! Don't get wise! Are you forgetting something?" Melvin patted his coat pocket. "I'm not afraid to use this."

"Mr. Shore…" the waitress interjected behind him. The sound from the Tiki Room clamored in.

"I know! I'm coming." He pointed at Marconi,

"Soon as you free that wise guy tinman, you two meet me out there. Your table's still reserved. This time take notes, okay? I need constructive criticism." He let the cooler door shut behind him.

Marconi groaned, "Oh Cronco, please tell me you've planned an escape for us."

"I was thinking of knocking down that wall."

"Well, I for one won't stop you."

The big robot took a step towards the wall. They were surrounded by shelves, frozen bags and boxes, when a splashing sound made them turn around. It came from the tall wooden vat behind them. They hadn't paid it any mind before, not until something stirred in it and a hand gripped the rim above. A woman pulled herself up enough to see them.

"You don't want to go through that wall," she said. "You'll fall right into the lake."

Marconi was genuinely surprised. He gasped, "Who are you?"

"I'm Aphrodite," she said. "I'm on later, after laughing boy. They pull me out in a glass tank and I do some mermaid tricks for the faithful. I overheard you say you're looking for a goldfish?"

Marconi said, "Yes, that's correct. A black and

white goldfish."

"Perhaps it's the same one I'm looking for," she said. "I've been wondering where he got to. The last time I saw him was at the Athens Hotel."

Marconi chattered, "My dear, that's the very fish we've been searching for! My comrade Cronco here has a good lead on his whereabouts. We could have investigated the lair of that unfortunate inventor had it not been for Melvin Shore's brazen coercion."

"Oh brother." She ran a hand through her green hair, "Let me guess, did he pull a space-gun on you?"

"He did indeed."

She rolled her eyes. "Not that gag again. He never changes his material. Okay, I'll get you out of your predicament if you tell me more about that goldfish."

"Deal!" Marconi rubbed his hands together. "Anything to get out of this glacier!"

She reached from the water and put her hand on a lever next to her tank. She smiled, "You might want to watch what happens out there on stage."

"Gladly," Marconi hurried for the door with Cronco wheezing after.

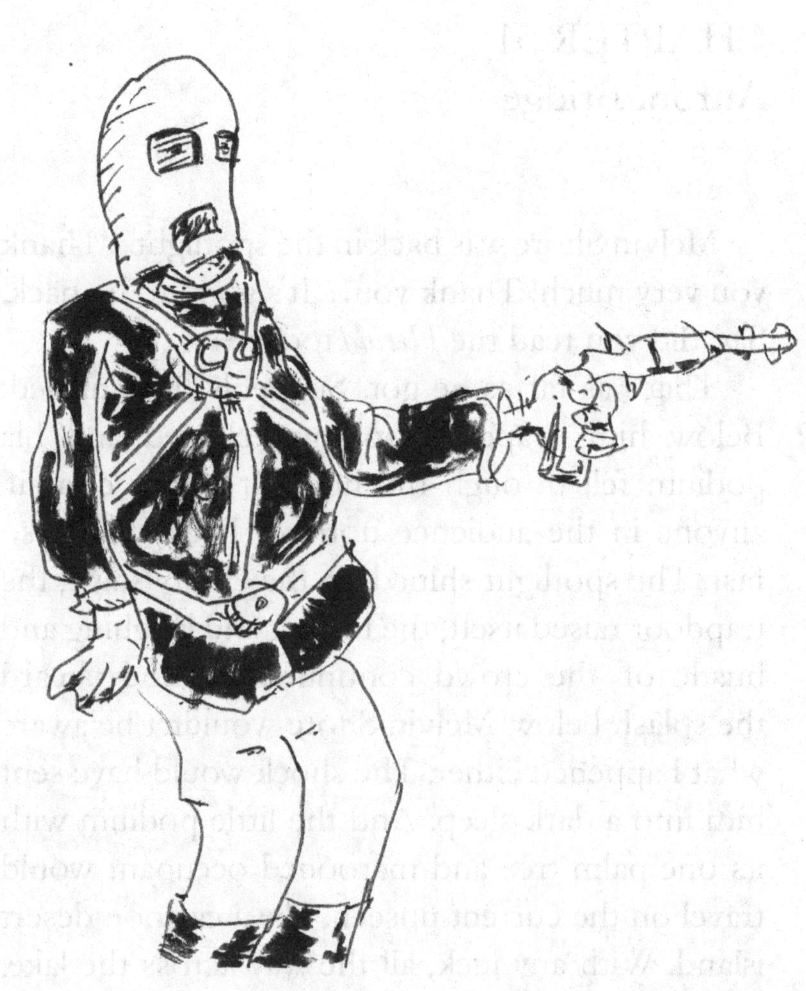

CHAPTER 31
Aurora Bridge

Melvin Shore was back in the spotlight. "Thank you very much! Thank you…It's good to be back. Say, did you read the *Herald* today?"

That's as far as he got. Suddenly he vanished. Below him, trapdoor springs released and his podium fell through the floor. It wasn't clear if anyone in the audience noticed. It happened so fast. The spotlight shined on the empty stage, the trapdoor raised itself, the talking and laughing and bustle of the crowd continued. Nobody heard the splash below. Melvin Shore wouldn't be aware what happened either. The shock would have sent him into a dark sleep. And the little podium with its one palm tree and marooned occupant would travel on the current unseen, like a cartoon desert island. With any luck, all the way across the lake, he would float to Union Bay, under the Montlake

Bridge, into Portage Bay past the university, further past Gas Works Park, with the light of dawn on the curved beams of Aurora Bridge and the ship canal, past docks, marinas, across Salmon Bay, with the water turning salty, through the locks of Commodore Way, and at last delivered to the sea.

CHAPTER 32
Along the Voyage

I know what it's like to need the Counterfeit Reality machine, to see someone you dearly miss. One time I asked Neptune about this. I wanted to know if I could contact my wife. Is there somewhere people go when they die, and would they stay the same way you knew them, even after they were gone for thirty years? Neptune said of course that place exists, he could take me on a narrow boat along the River Styx where the dead lined the shores like driftwood. I said let's go. I didn't even know what I would say. I had no idea what would happen. Our narrow boat slowed. I was so young when she left me alone. I didn't know how to process that death. In a way I think I let it kill me too, or at least it tried to. I became as lost as I've ever been. I think I wanted to tell her what she did to me, what drowning in the harbor had done, but she didn't need to know that—I was the one who was haunted by that legacy, she was just a girl in her twenties whose job now was to make the stars shine. There are people we miss, that's a fact, and maybe it's best to leave it that way, part of what we lose along the voyage that makes us who we are. I begged Neptune to turn us around. I wasn't ready to see her yet.

That's the sort of machine we're dealing with in this book.

I didn't need imagination to know the danger I was in.

I woke early so I could get to Spoon's house before Marconi and Cronco did. I have no desire to meet them in person, I'd rather they stay two dimensional. On paper, I can handle them. Hearing them on the telephone, seeing them on television, it gets strange—anything more real than that and I might succumb.

I wasn't sure how it would go spiriting Neptune out of the aquarium, away. I brought a paper cup in my coat pocket. I figured I would look for a chance to scoop him out.

CHAPTER 33
Daydreaming

I didn't go round back to Santy's Upholstery, I went straight to the front door of the house and knocked. Just as expected, I met the twin and was let into the waiting room with its paintings, magazines, chairs, and an empty fish tank. That figures, doesn't it. "Where are the fish?" I asked. I walked up to the glass to see if they were hiding in the castle with the drawbridge pulled up. There was no answer though. I was alone. I was in a waiting room all alone with my thoughts.

It occurred to me, what if Marconi and Cronco beat me to this room and the aquarium and Neptune? They seemed determined to do that, it was possible, especially with Aphrodite's help. Did they haul her mermaid tank here from Lake City Way? Wouldn't I have noticed it, parked in the lot with the cars. I pictured Cronco holding a rope, tirelessly pulling the fish tank, Marconi telling the mermaid stories, arriving at Spoon's at 4 A.M. with the skyline rim running gold. The birds in this neighborhood would've been awake, maybe Coach Wooden would go past slow, headlights, surprised by the sight. By that time, I imagined Marconi asleep on the back of the wagon, his shoes scuffing along the sidewalk, top hat down over his face.

When Feldspar Spoon appeared in the waiting room, I was still daydreaming. I can fill pages that way.

It may seem like I have control of the world I write about, but it turns out I was wrong about the goldfish plot. Spoon told me what happened. We went to the nursery and he showed me the Counterfeit Reality machine. It didn't resemble the atom bomb or some other thing that could make so much trouble. It was just a movie projector and a screen but look what it could do. Spoon promised it wouldn't take us where Eel went, not anymore. He reset it. It could never go there again.

He erased its memory of the bank on Magnolia Street by planting a new memory in its place. He said it was a simple operation, he spun a dial on the side of the projector and ran the view of town across the screen until it showed a beautiful green pond in the Japanese Garden at the Arboretum. Spoon said he had to give something back to the world after what he had done. That's what happened to the eight goldfish in the waiting room. He carried them to the nursery and reached his arm into the glimmering light of the projector and poured Neptune and the rest of them in.

Then something happened I didn't expect. Spoon said Cronco opened his hatch and I've already stated so many times what he carries in there it should be obvious, or so I thought, until he reached a claw inside and showed Spoon what swam in a glass of water. The robot asked if Spoon could send another goldfish to that pond too.

I knew who it was. There was no need to drag a mermaid tank through town. Aphrodite could change herself just like Neptune. They both had power over water.

So that's where they are. A pond in a garden beautiful as Eden. Neptune must be happy being a fish, people just keep complicating things. And Aphrodite was happy that way too.

CHAPTER 34
Living in Water

I don't think anyone would believe that it's been Neptune all along who has been my muse. All this time, all these books, he was nearby for me to write. But Neptune has never been gone so long. Now that he's been away for days, maybe always, I find I'm still able to write, in fact the writing seems to have taken on a life of its own. It's an unbroken flow. All I need is faith, to think of him, to know that he exists somewhere, anywhere, apparently he's everywhere.

No, not everywhere, that's not true. There are a lot of us, and the oceans and rivers and lakes cover the planet. Neptune can't be everywhere all the time, but I can assure you that this god does care about us and keeps an eye on us. Sometimes you might doubt it but it's true. Having direct contact with God, I can honestly say knowing this is a comfort beyond words.

I came back home and sat at the typewriter and the words find me so easily. Here are some more. There's a lot to share. And guess what? I'm not ready for Neptune's book to end quite yet. I'm going to write it the way I want. Forget about Spoon and what he said happened. Everyone deserves their own reality. Let's go back to early morning. We're starting again. That's right, I'm rewriting it. Why not? This is my fictional account of something that was already fiction to begin with.

Marconi and Cronco are out there looking for Neptune. Not that they know they're searching for a Roman god, they just think he's a goldfish. But they seem to be doing alright, they're on the trail. They will still get to Spoon's before me and he will tell them where he sent the fish and I'm sure they'll find their way to the Japanese Garden to get him and if Neptune's not there swimming around, they'll find clues to where he went next. They might keep looking forever. Take a look at the globe, give it a spin, living in water you can end up nearly anywhere.

CHAPTER 35
The Law of the Jungle

A bit after 10 A.M, Marconi and Cronco arrived at Feldspar Spoon's quiet house. There was no answer when they knocked on the door, no twin, and the door wasn't locked so they let themselves in. Marconi bustled ahead, straight for the fish tank. He had a coffee mug in his hand and was prepared to wrangle that lost pet in. Finding the aquarium empty of fish was not what he expected. Marconi was frantically searching around the base of the table when Cronco sidled up to him.

"They're gone, Cronco! Every one of them!" the magician wailed. "Vanished!"

Cronco parked on the carpet and hummed.

"No sign of them," Marconi got back to his feet and drummed fingers on his forehead. "Maybe Spoon brought them into the other room? He might be painting them."

"Painting goldfish?" Cronco said. "That seems impractical."

"*Making* a painting of them, Cronco," Marconi replied. "The man is an artist! Look around!"

Cronco whistled something audible only in the ultrasonic range—a dog three blocks away lifted its head quizzically—then he shuffled his two iron left feet after Marconi.

Instead of dog frequency, what Marconi heard as he neared the next room was a familiar raised voice. He froze and put a hand up to stop the robot behind him. "The gangster is back!" he hissed, "Retreat!"

True, Nick the Eel had escaped from jail. They didn't call him the eel for having a lackadaisical nature. If there were bars, he'd squeeze out—if there was a locked door, he would fashion a key.

"They're after me," the criminal snarled. "I need somewhere to go where they'll never find me."

Feldspar Spoon was still trying to calm his heart. He had quite a jolt when the convict burst in. At least Nick the Eel wasn't vengeful. Thankfully. Spoon was well aware that people ended up wearing concrete shoes, doing time in the bay for betraying a gangster. Nervously, he tried to convince Nick there was a malfunction, how he did everything he could to get him back from the bank, but Nick didn't care about that. It was old news.

Eel demanded, "I want you to send me somewhere. I want to be with my cat, I don't want to be here no more."

That surprised Feldspar. No client ever wanted to stay in that projection with their pet. They shed tears of joy with the reunion, some ache in their heart was repaired knowing that other place existed like heaven behind a curtain. Then they said goodbye, aware of two things: their pet was alright, and that when it was their time they would be there too. Meanwhile, they still had their lives to live in this counterfeit reality.

But Nick the Eel was desperate. He was done with America and the law of the jungle. "What do you say, professor?"

Spoon pondered, "I guess we can do that…I have your information on file…your cat's coordinates are entered in my logbook…"

"Well, what are we waiting for?" Nick barked.

"Okay," Spoon said, "Right away." He kept the logbook on the shelf next to a Dr. Seuss book, along with a lot of dust and the circular print where a tin can had been. He pulled it down and paged through. "Let's see…" Had he filed it under 'Eel' or 'Nick'?

CHAPTER 36
Balloon Animals

Marconi and Cronco live in a tall apartment with a stairway that runs up through the center. You can stand on the ground floor of the stairwell shaft and view all the way to the small square of ceiling, floors and floors above. Some strange brilliant-colored creatures huddle up there, unable to go further they bump numbly about.

Just a few weeks ago, before they took on The Case of the Wayward Goldfish, Marconi had a job selling balloons. Each day he would come down the stairs with a big bouquet, on his journey to the zoo. He wasn't very good at making balloon animals, he couldn't make a giraffe or elephant, but he found a way to sell the awkward creatures he bent and formed. He would spend the day outside the Martian animal cages and hawk his balloon curiosities there. After you saw a Dustbeagle, a

Brainee, or a Raving Snowpop, his balloons looked meant to be.

Each morning when Cronco and he would clang down the stairs, it was five stories down from their apartment, he lost a few balloons along the way. They floated free, against gravity, up, up, up, where they wanted to go, towards outer space where a certain red planet would be glad to welcome them home.

CHAPTER 37
Greta Garbo

Marconi rushed right over the envelope as he scurried across the floor of their apartment. He still imagined Nick the Eel hot on their heels. He didn't notice the letter, but Cronco did.

Cronco felt the shifting cargo inside his compartment, the goldfish flyer, the half-empty cracker box, two tin cans, the spare sparkplug, Baroness Pannonia's personal card, and the letter from the Department of Internal Revenue, as he bent to retrieve the envelope. He scanned it. It was another letter from the Department of Internal Revenue. This one was stamped URGENT.

Cronco held it in his claw as he glanced at Marconi. The old man lay collapsed in his chair by the window, eyes tightly closed, feet up on a tuffet. Their wild escape home had tired him out. All he needed was rest and calm to catch his breath. What a sight…Cronco wondered what would happen if he was paired with someone daring and dashing instead, someone like Errol Flynn or Maureen O'Sullivan. A robot like Cronco had dreams and accomplishments to achieve.

Cronco might have gone to recharge at the outlet in his usual corner near the kitchen window. He didn't. His sensors alerted him that someone was at the door. A second later there was a knock and he went to answer it. Imagine, Cronco steamed, a #501322, the most advanced automaton of its day, relegated to butler duties.

A telegram delivery robot leaned against the door jamb and almost fell in. "Brother…" it wheezed, "That's a lot of stairs…" It presented Cronco with a sealed telegram. "Good news though—I couldn't help giving it a scan—keeps the job lively," he winked. "You'll be pleased with this."

Cronco examined the address on the telegram. A third notice from the Department of Internal Revenue!

"I'm still waiting for my notice," the delivery robot said wistfully.

Cronco fished a coin from his metal wallet and

handed it over.

"Thanks pal," the other robot tipped his blue visored hat. "Until next time, best of luck to you."

Not only was Cronco equipped with ultrasonic transmitters, he was also able to generate gamma rays in the electromagnetic spectrum, making the sealed telegram in his claw readable. His silent reaction was on loan from Greta Garbo. Softly as celluloid, he crackled and turned slowly and marched over to the magician snoring in his chair.

CHAPTER 38
Servitude

Marconi held both the urgent envelope and the new telegram while Cronco retrieved the other letter from his compartment. The robot had known all along what was written. The waiting was over.

"Well, they certainly are persistent," Marconi said. He reached in his tuxedo and with all the aplomb he could muster got his reading glasses and a handkerchief. He cleaned the lenses before he put them on. "Let's see…where should I begin?"

"They all say the same thing," Cronco told him.

Marconi eyed him suspiciously.

Cronco shrugged.

"Alright then, I'll open the telegram." Marconi held it up to the daylight. He paused before tearing the seam. "You needn't stand there observing me, Cronco. I'm not the Great Gildersleeve." Mumbling to himself, he read the message. His reaction was less Greta Garbo and more Una Merkel. Flustered, he quickly opened the urgent letter. Then he took off his glasses and rubbed his eyes. "Maybe I'm still dreaming…" he sighed. He opened his eyes. The letters remained on his lap. "Alas, I am not." Restoring his glasses, Marconi read aloud:

"We found an error on your Form 1040, which affects the following area of your return: Robot Rebate Recovery Credit. The error was in one or more of the following: The Social Security number of one or more robots claimed as a qualifying dependent was missing, incomplete, or inapplicable. One or more robots claimed as a qualifying dependent exceeds the servitude limit. The robot rebate credit was incorrectly applied. Therefore we changed your return to correct this error. As a result, you are no longer able to claim a robot as your dependent and must immediately comply with its emancipation."

Marconi refolded the letter. He said, "You know, we've been partners for a long time."

"Affirmative."

"Well…Don't get me wrong, my good fellow, I had no idea this rule applied. Apparently your freedom has been granted. Your services in my company are no longer required." He rattled the three notices he clutched, "You have been given your walking papers." He stood and turned to look out the window. "I've always appreciated your friendship. You've been invaluable as a partner in magic and mystery. It's a shame that our final enterprise, the lost goldfish assignment, will remain unsolved…" Above the Leopold building floated a fish-shaped raincloud. There were more swimming after. When it rained, it poured.

CHAPTER 39
Santa Monica

Feldspar Spoon's next client also arrived unannounced. There was no doubt who it was. The hallway shook and creaked with the thudding approach of White Pongo. A painting of a windmill tilted on the wall. Funny, Spoon didn't hear the commotion. He seemed entranced, staring at the pale, lifeless screen across from him. The projector was turned off. Nick the Eel was in there, disappeared. Spoon was wondering if the right thing had been done letting him go. Or was this just the beginning of a migration to other worlds? Spoon frowned. Was he tipping the universe on end? Should he be done with it, should he turn the projector back on and toss it into the screen, into some prehistoric land before time where nobody would find it? A dinosaur could step on it, that would be fine.

Then what? Make room for another reality. Spoon could turn the house into a neighborhood gallery. He could try to make it as an artist. And even if that didn't pan out, he still had the upholstery business. He could keep fixing car seats and benches and chairs, people always needed that.

That's when the gorilla threw the nursery door open and snorted heavily. The shiny buttons on his snug uniform threatened to bullet the room.

"Oh!" Spoon turned. "Good afternoon. Or whatever part of day or night we're in."

Pongo pointed at the movie screen and slapped his heart.

"I know, I know..." Spoon hated to see the poor gorilla throw his money away week after week. How much did he make as a bellhop anyway? Not much. Probably not enough to pay a decent rent, he probably had room in a broom closet, or slept in a tree on the hotel lot. What kind of life was that?

As Spoon activated the machine, he told Pongo, "I have an idea." He didn't have to get the logbook, he didn't need coordinates, by now he had memorized where Pongo needed to go. And it occurred to him, maybe he could make his living this way—sending the lonely and misplaced into better worlds. Why give them a window when they could enter a door and leave?

The screen came alive with the sunshine of a beautiful California. You could almost feel the warm breeze moving the orange flowers and butterflies. Santa Monica was nice. It wasn't the Congo, but her garden was a gorilla's dream. Pongo's eyes were fixed on someone in the center of all that green, a woman at a table, reading a book, a small paperback *Walt Amherst is Awake*. Pongo stepped closer and his shoulders brushed against the stream of light, making shadow on the screen, something cool, like when a cloud momentarily touches the sun.

Pamela felt it. She looked away from her book. She stared out of the screen. "White Pongo? Is that you?" How could he appear like that in the air? Did she wish him real? "It is you, isn't it?" She held up a hand reaching for him. After all those years ago running from him, now she wanted him.

"Go on," Spoon urged him. "You can be with her forever."

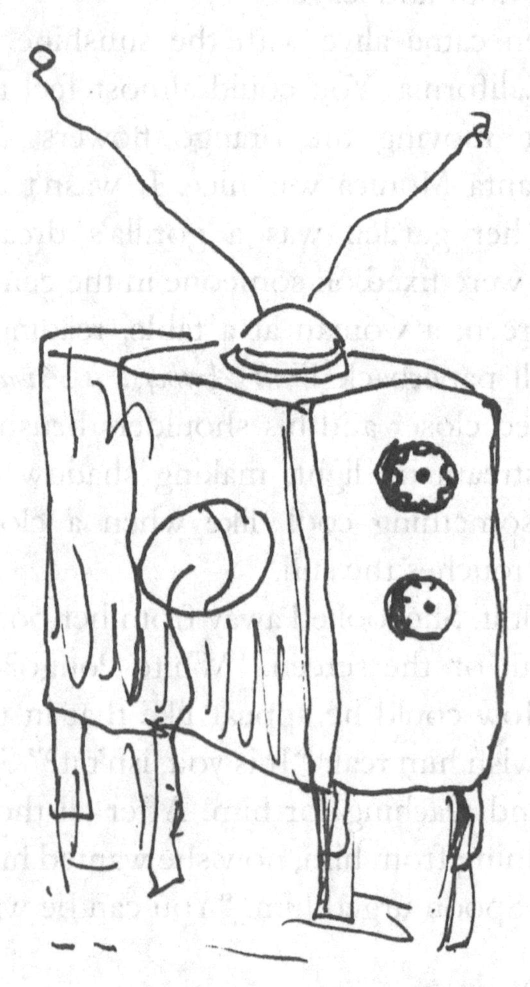

CHAPTER 40
Neptune's Warning

Thankfully, there was no sign of Marconi or Cronco in tonight's *June on the Moon*. They were back in the stack of pages by the typewriter. Frankly, I didn't expect to see them again. Now that Cronco had his freedom, he could draw tourists on the boulevard, or work for the Baroness Pannonia in her mansion by the sea. That was fine with me. Marconi could go back to selling balloons, or walking dogs, or magic shows, or special guest on TV. They weren't my concern.

Nonetheless, I caught myself thinking of them while I was washing dishes. I quickly made myself think of something else.

This book is nearly done. I haven't seen Neptune again. Does it matter? I gave him a book where he lurks about. That's what he wanted. Wasn't that enough? We're a long way from Roman days. This is no longer a time of wars and discord, ignorance and conspiracy, where thunder and lightning are feared, where the rising, falling seas are a mystery, and there is depthless need to pray to something bigger than us. That's ancient history. Neptune. I have mentioned his name throughout, what more praise can a god expect?

The phone rang. I dried off my hands and answered it. It figures….It was Neptune.

Rain beaded on the dark kitchen window above the sink. Neptune was free to move about in human form, a very old man with a trident for a cane. He was calling me from a phonebooth on Pacific Street. In the background I could hear the car tires sizzling.

He asked me what I was doing. I told him I was trying to wrap it up. I told him the plot, I made my case for the story so far, I explained how it was a metaphorical search for an unseeable, unknowable god. I said this would make a good ending, us talking on the telephone, me promising that as long as I've told my story well, people will know that Neptune is still out there walking in the rain.

He told me that's not what he meant. There

was a far more important task. He said something was wrong, there was a disturbance in the balance of things mortal and celestial. I had to take the receiver from my ear while he roared like the sea in a seashell.

I looked at the rain coming down lit by the streetlamp outside. I had a pretty good idea what concerned him. Call it an author's intuition. I guessed he meant the Counterfeit Reality machine. I don't know when Neptune became aware of its existence, he didn't take a lot of interest in machines, he preferred walking in the water. Hesitantly, I brought up the subject of Feldspar Spoon and that invention.

That was it alright. Neptune warned me no living being could be marooned in the heavenly realms. He saw cracks in pillars, signs and omens. Neptune feared some catastrophe was sure to ensue and he told me what had to be done, what I had to do.

CHAPTER 41
Whirlpool

So much for the end of the book. Looks like it won't be happening yet, and it certainly isn't the way I planned. Neptune didn't give me rules carved in stone to carry back to town, but his command sent me like a sleepwalker into the rain. It took me fifteen minutes to get to Spoon's house. I wasn't proud of what I had to do, but I couldn't exactly refuse orders from a god.

Creeping along the side of Spoon's house like ivy, careful of the flowers, I reached for the window. The rain helped to muffle the sound of me putting a foot in the rhododendron. I pulled myself up over the sill and then I was inside. Fortunately, it was a room I had been in before, it hadn't changed, except that now it was filled with gloom. I saw the empty aquarium.

I squeaked across the floor, dripping, leaving

a trail on the way to the nursery. This sounds like I've become the Creature of the Black Lagoon but let me be clear: I would state in court should I be caught, that I don't consider myself guilty of any wrongdoing. I'm no Nick the Eel. I could even call on God as a witness, provided the bailiff had a goldfish bowl.

The nursery door fanned opened quietly and I snuck into the room, drawing a flashlight from my raincoat like Sam Spade. In the shadows, the projector was a dim silhouette. I never got to watch the Counterfeit Reality machine in use, but I figured the controls wouldn't be too difficult. When I shone the flashlight on its surface, I was pleased to see a simple START button. I don't know how it works, if there were settings that glowed from here to other realities, it didn't matter. My instructions from Neptune were straightforward. I was to turn the projector on and throw it into whatever world it appeared. Then it would be gone, sucked into its own whirlpool.

So, I pressed the START button.

Ahead of me the movie screen filled with moonlight. It shimmered in the room like a square of fog. I was supposed to be quick and follow the plan, but the picture on the screen was subtly changing, tantalizing, becoming a shape of something forming in cloudiness.

As soon as I recognized her, I forgot all about this reality.

It didn't occur to me until much later that Neptune knew what he was doing, sending me into a movie. Imagine the odds of all the counterfeit realities where I could be. Only with a god's help could I land in the right one.

From the screen, my wife called my name and I walked right into those rays, carrying the machine in my arms like a baby.

CHAPTER 42
In a Blue Rowboat

Words go on without me, as they always do, we all take turns living here, only someone like Neptune is never-ending. I bowed out when I jumped into the counterfeit reality machine.

Something was left behind though, unlikely as it seems. My last dream showed up on Feldspar Spoon's billboard that night. And maybe if people paid attention, maybe it would have made a difference, maybe not. The next day things were going to happen no matter what.

The billboard leans against Lincoln Street, pushing on the piles of blackberry, facing the highway, all the cars driving past. During the day, tall words and pictures are printed on it, the usual advertisements for better cars and other products you commonly see, but as soon as night falls, the billboard becomes a drive-in movie screen showing dreams. Everyone sleeping could be the lucky star—it's surprising it took so long to find me!

There's a usual crowd that watches the billboard every night. In their own way they're just as eager to see movies as I used to be, going to the Neptune Theatre. They pull up lawn chairs along the side of the road. People bring pillows and blankets and refreshments. Cars passing by get a brief glimpse of a haunted window. Feldspar Spoon invented one of the great wonders of the night sky.

Miraculously, Spoon's machine caught me on my way out the door. My life must have left just enough in the air to be projected on the billboard.

Here's what it showed:

My wife and I were afloat in a blue rowboat. The whole town waved below us. Everything was familiar but not the same, everything was underwater. Everyone was in Neptune's realm. The monorail eeled along its track. Between houses with windows lit like Halloween pumpkins, birds flew like schools of fish. I could see backyards, kids climbing trees on branches of waving kelp. I pointed at our house and asked her if we were in there, different but the same, accustomed to water, living in a counterfeit world.

Coach Wooden was still steamed about having to dump all that bad Neptune water the other night, but he couldn't risk it poisoning his stock. Even if this was only a prank thought up by his rival, a tape-recorded message, or a radio signal directed at him, it left him with a bad taste. Worst of all, it was unsportsmanlike conduct. You had to play by rules.

The radio was on, the Oakland As were playing in a field of cottony static that came and went from the open cab. He was getting ready for his dawn run, down Milk Street where the dairy trucks would be beginning theirs too.

Wooden Water came from a natural spring underground. Coach set his crates next to the faucet. He turned the handle and waited for the first bottle to fill. Wherever you go, America is a land of what used to be, and long ago is linked to today. The Coach's backyard was once a campground for the circus when they passed through. They drew water from the spring for their animals and sold it bottled as Miracle Water at night. That's where Coach Wooden got the idea for his empire, at the circus, watching the clowns hand out bottles. He was just a freckled kid who liked to toss the ball, but one day he would do the same circus game.

The faucet sputtered and the water stopped.

Coach growled and got to his knees. An owl hooted in the dark, clashing with the radio. He unlatched the padlocked wooden hatch on the ground and pushed it aside. Descending into the earth wasn't uncommon for him. More and more it was happening. Somewhere the suction got knotted or pinched by a rock. Not hard to fix, not when you're prepared. Back in the truck he kept a miner's hat and a gym rope. They were pushed under the seat.

Only the brightest stars and planets could be seen in the wash of city skyglow.

When he got behind the steering wheel, he rested, sat and listened to the game. He never tired of the magic. He was able to picture what was happening on that field in faraway California night. If only he was coaching that team, he knew what he'd do. He'd bolt from the dugout and hit that stadium green light, waving his arms like a traffic cop. If only that wasn't fantasy, his imagination at play. He had more important things to do.

He got his helmet, flicked the lantern switch and settled the hat on his crewcut. The coliseum continued without him. He wouldn't find out who would win. Coach Wooden left the cab and splashed in the ghoulish light of the headlamp. It was a little spooky this early, not that Coach Wooden was scared. There was nothing to be afraid of. By morning this would be a different world, bright with birds and rabbits. Beside of the open hatch he tied his rope to a cleat and tossed the loops down ahead of him.

It's worth mentioning that Coach Wooden could have given all this up, he could have retired to a simple quiet life, got interested in some hobby like putting ships in all those bottles. He could sit by the window and write messages on three hundred sails and send them out to sea. Words could have been his water. But he was never one to sit idly by, he gave life a hundred ten percent. There was no sign of him in the yard, he was already twenty feet gone.

The radio announcer was sorry to report Martinez struck out and the inning was over and, "We'll be right back after this message from your local station." It was a commercial for sweet peach jam, "good on toast, good on a cracker, good on anything you put it on" and the cheery voice ended in a song, "Take it from me and the fruit on the tree, pectin's where it's at!"

Suddenly a geyser shot from the ground, a wide jet of water reaching a hundred feet in the air. Who knew there was so much Wooden Water? It was the beginning of a new inland sea.

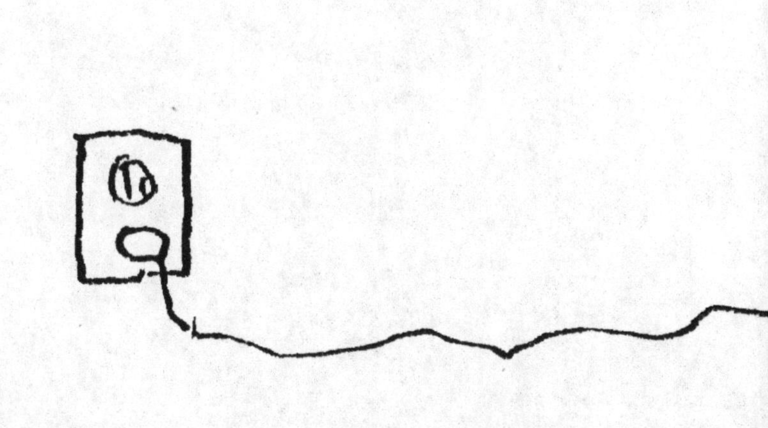

CHAPTER 44
Calypso

The oars have gone idle. The storm has passed, the air is a hush, calm water, safe and inviting to put a hand in and trail along, tracing the rooftops and parks and streets of the Atlantis below. Across from us, the old hills are new islands raised above the waves. Green cedar trees, blue skies. I wish I could gather everyone here to see, but there's only room for two. Just us, and a mouse named Calypso, floating past on a plank of wood.

NEPTUNALIA

Written spring through summer of 2022.
First draft finished August 15, roofers hammering
next door.
Second draft finished November 18, 2022, with
The Beatles "in the land of submarines."

Aaron Gunderson illustration from
A Field of Cabbages (2020)

Books by Good Deed Rain

Saint Lemonade, Allen Frost, 2014. Two novels illustrated by the author in the manner of the old Big Little Books.

Playground, Allen Frost, 2014. Poems collected from seven years of chapbooks.

Roosevelt, Allen Frost, 2015. A Pacific Northwest novel set in July, 1942, when a boy and a girl search for a missing elephant. Illustrated throughout by Fred Sodt.

5 Novels, Allen Frost, 2015. Novels written over five years, featuring circus giants, clockwork animals, detectives and time travelers.

The Sylvan Moore Show, Allen Frost, 2015. A short story omnibus of 193 stories written over 30 years.

Town in a Cloud, Allen Frost, 2015. A three-part book of poetry, written during the Bellingham rainy seasons of fall, winter, and spring.

A Flutter of Birds Passing Through Heaven: A Tribute to Robert Sund, 2016. Edited by Allen Frost and Paul Piper. The story of a legendary Ish River poet & artist.

At the Edge of America, Allen Frost, 2016. Two novels in one book blend time travel in a mythical poetic America.

Lake Erie Submarine, Allen Frost, 2016. A two week vacation in Ohio inspired these poems, illustrated by the author.

and Light, Paul Piper, 2016. Poetry written over three years. Illustrated with watercolors by Penny Piper.

The Book of Ticks, Allen Frost, 2017. A giant collection of 8 mysterious adventures featuring Phil Ticks. Illustrated throughout by Aaron Gunderson.

I Can Only Imagine, Allen Frost, 2017. Five adventures of love and heartbreak dreamed in an imaginary world. Cover & color illustrations by Annabelle Barrett.

The Orphanage of Abandoned Teenagers, Allen Frost, 2017. A fictional guide for teens and their parents. Illustrated by the author.

In the Valley of Mystic Light: An Oral History of the Skagit Valley Arts Scene, 2017. A comprehensive illustrated tribute. Edited by Claire Swedberg & Rita Hupy.

Different Planet, Allen Frost, 2017. Four science fiction adventures: reincarnation, robots, talking animals, outer space and clones. Illustrated by Laura Vasyutynska.

Go with the Flow: A Tribute to Clyde Sanborn, 2018. Edited by Allen Frost. The life and art of a timeless river poet. In beautiful living color!

Homeless Sutra, Allen Frost, 2018. Four stories: Sylvan Moore, a flying monk, a water salesman, and a guardian rabbit.

The Lake Walker, Allen Frost 2018. A little novel set in black and white like one of those old European movies about death and life.

A Hundred Dreams Ago, Allen Frost, 2018. A winter book of poetry and prose. Illustrated by Aaron Gunderson.

Almost Animals, Allen Frost, 2018. A collection of linked stories, thinking about what makes us animals.

The Robotic Age, Allen Frost, 2018. A vaudeville magician and his faithful robot track down ghosts. Illustrated throughout by Aaron Gunderson.

Kennedy, Allen Frost, 2018. This sequel to *Roosevelt* is a coming-of-age fable set during two weeks in 1962 in a mythical Kennedyland. Illustrated throughout by Fred Sodt.

Fable, Allen Frost, 2018. There's something going on in this country and I can best relate it in fable: the parable of the rabbits, a bedtime story, and the diary of our trip to Ohio.

Elbows & Knees: Essays & Plays, Allen Frost, 2018. A thrilling collection of writing about some of my favorite subjects, from B-movies to Brautigan.

The Last Paper Stars, Allen Frost 2019. A trip back in time to the 20 year old mind of Frankenstein, and two other worlds of the future.

Walt Amherst is Awake, Allen Frost, 2019. The dreamlife of an office worker. Illustrated throughout by Aaron Gunderson.

When You Smile You Let in Light, Allen Frost, 2019. An atomic love story written by a 23 year old.

Pinocchio in America, Allen Frost, 2019. After 82 years buried underground, Pinocchio returns to life behind a car repair shop in America.

Taking Her Sides on Immortality, Robert Huff, 2019. The long awaited poetry collection from a local, nationally renowned master of words.

Florida, Allen Frost, 2019. Three days in Florida turned into a book of sunshine inspired stories.

Blue Anthem Wailing, Allen Frost, 2019. My first novel written in college is an apocalyptic, Old Testament race through American shadows while Amelia Earhart flies overhead.

The Welfare Office, Allen Frost, 2019. The animals go in and out of the office, leaving these stories as footprints.

Island Air, Allen Frost, 2019. A detective novel featuring haiku, a lost library book and streetsongs.

Imaginary Someone, Allen Frost, 2020. A fictional memoir featuring 45 years of inspirations and obstacles in the life of a writer.

Violet of the Silent Movies, Allen Frost, 2020. A collection of starry-eyed short story poems, illustrated by the author.

The Tin Can Telephone, Allen Frost, 2020. A childhood memory novel set in 1975 Seattle, illustrated by author.

Heaven Crayon, Allen Frost, 2020. How the author's first book *Ohio Trio* would look if printed as a Big Little Book. Illustrated by the author.

Old Salt, Allen Frost, 2020. Authors of a fake novel get chased by tigers. Illustrations by the author.

A Field of Cabbages, Allen Frost, 2020. The sequel to *The Robotic Age* finds our heroes in a race against time to save Sunny Jim's ghost. Illustrated by Aaron Gunderson.

River Road, Allen Frost, 2020. A paperboy delivers the news to a ghost town. Illustrated by the author.

The Puttering Marvel, Allen Frost, 2021. Eleven short stories with illustrations by the author.

Something Bright, Allen Frost, 2021. 106 short story poems walking with you from winter into spring. Illustrated by the author.

The Trillium Witch, Allen Frost, 2021. A detective novel about witches in the Pacific Northwest rain. Illustrated by the author.

Cosmonaut, Allen Frost, 2021. Yuri Gagarin's rocket lands in America. Midnight jazz, folk music, mystery and sorcery. Illustrated by the author.

Thriftstore Madonna, Allen Frost, 2021. 124 summer story poems. Illustrated by the author.

Half a Giraffe, Allen Frost, 2021. A magical novel about a counterfeiter and his unusual, beloved pet. Illustrated by the author.

Lexington Brown & The Pond Projector, Allen Frost, 2022. An underwater invention takes three friends through time. Illustrated by Aaron Gunderson.

The Robert Huck Museum, Allen Frost, 2022. The artist's life story told in photographs, woodcuts, paintings, prints and drawings.

Mrs. Magnusson & Friends, Allen Frost, 2022. A collection of 13 stories featuring mystery and ginkgo leaves.

Magic Island, Allen Frost, 2022. There's a memory machine in this magical novel that takes us to college.

A Red Leaf Boat, Allen Frost, 2022. Inspired by Japan, this book of 142 poems is the result of walking in autumn.

Forest & Field, Allen Frost, 2022. 117 forest and field recordings made during the summer months, ending with a lullaby.

The Wires and Circuits of Earth, Allen Frost, 2022. 11 stories from a train station pulp magazine.

The Air Over Paris, Allen Frost, 2023. This novel reveals the truth about semi-sentient speedbumps from Mars.

Neptunalia, Allen Frost, 2023. A movie-novel for Neptune, featuring mystery in a Counterfeit Reality machine. Illustrated by Aaron Gunderson.

Books by Bottom Dog Press

Ohio Trio, Allen Frost, 2001. Three short novels written in magic fields and small towns of Ohio. Reprinted as *Heaven Crayon* in 2020.

Bowl of Water, Allen Frost, 2004. Poetry. From the glass factory to when you wake up.

Another Life, Allen Frost, 2007. Poetry. From the last Ohio morning to the early bird.

Home Recordings, Allen Frost, 2009. Poetry. Dream machinery, filming Caruso, benign time travel.

The Mermaid Translation, Allen Frost, 2010. A bathysphere novel with Philip Marlowe.

Selected Correspondence of Kenneth Patchen, Edited by Larry Smith and Allen Frost, 2012. Amazing artist letters.

The Wonderful Stupid Man, Allen Frost, 2012. Short stories. go from Aristotle's first car to the 500 dollar fool.

9 781088 084441